“We’re going to find her.”

Daniel said it again, more for his benefit than Annie’s. They had to. The other option—unacceptable.

Arms crossed, Annie dug her fingernails into her skin. “If someone hurt my little girl...”

Daniel looked at her. For a moment, the world fell away, and it was just the two of them. “They won’t. Not if I have anything to say about it.”

“I promised Libby that if anything happened to her and Austin, I’d protect Lily and keep her safe. Raise her right. Now this...” Annie spread her arms, palms up, and spun slowly in a circle. Her eyes combed the area. She fisted her hands. “Where is she? Where’s my daughter?”

For the first time since the nightmare had begun, Annie’s tears fell. The strong, determined woman she’d portrayed shattered.

Unable to stop himself, he gathered her in his arms and held her as fear and grief spilled from her eyes.

He couldn’t fail his best friend from his youth, and there was no way he could fail another child.

Award-winning, bestselling author **Sami A. Abrams** grew up hating to read. It wasn't until her thirties that she found authors who captured her attention. Most evenings, you can find her engrossed in a romantic suspense novel. She lives in Northern California but will always be a Kansas girl at heart. She has a love of sports, family and travel. However, writing her next story in a cabin at Lake Tahoe tops her list.

Books by Sami A. Abrams

Love Inspired Suspense

Tracking the Missing

Stone Creek Ranch

Christmas Rodeo Killer
Deadly Rodeo Threat
Rodeo Witness Protector

Deputies of Anderson County

Buried Cold Case Secrets
Twin Murder Mix-Up
Detecting Secrets
Killer Christmas Evidence
Witness Escape

Visit the Author Profile page at LoveInspired.com.

RODEO WITNESS PROTECTOR

SAMI A. ABRAMS

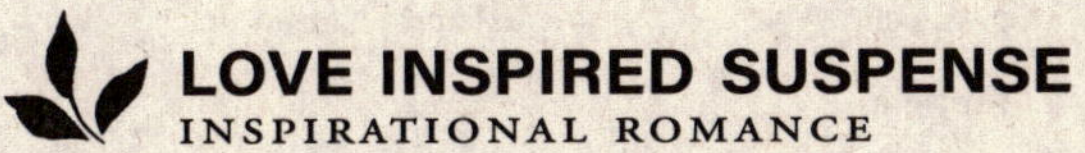

Recycling programs for this product may not exist in your area.

ISBN-13: 978-1-335-91908-3

Rodeo Witness Protector

For questions and comments about the quality of this book, please contact us at CustomerService@Harlequin.com.

Love Inspired
22 Adelaide St. West, 41st Floor
Toronto, Ontario M5H 4E3, Canada
www.LoveInspired.com

HarperCollins Publishers
Macken House, 39/40 Mayor Street Upper,
Dublin 1, D01 C9W8, Ireland
www.HarperCollins.com

Printed in Lithuania

1 2 3 4 5 6 7 8 9 10 LIT 28 27 26 25

Fear thou not; for I am with thee: be not dismayed;
for I am thy God: I will strengthen thee; yea, I will
help thee; yea, I will uphold thee with the right hand
of my righteousness.

—*Isaiah* 41:10

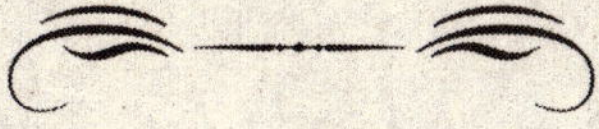

This book is dedicated to Michele Catlett.
I will never forget the phone calls and the laughs
that went along with them. I miss you, my friend.
Enjoy dancing with Jesus.

ONE

"He's out on bail, Annie." The words of Dr. Annie Davis's mentor, Dr. Todd Gregory, ratcheted her heart rate.

Annie clutched her new phone, stumbled back, and grasped the kitchen counter. She'd thanked God that the authorities had arrested Dr. Pope a few days ago. Due to the timing of the arrest and the weekend, she'd had five days to plan her escape. According to the court schedule, she had until tomorrow morning to pack her and her daughter Lily's things and get out of town—away from accusing stares—away from his threats on their lives. Dr. Pope shouldn't be able to find her. She hadn't returned to Rollins since her mother had moved her during high school. For all anyone knew, Houston was her home. Out of caution, she'd ditched her old phone number and purchased a pay-as-you-go phone. Only three people could contact her. Todd, her new boss, Donovan Keats, and the new babysitter, Karly. The plan to be long gone before Pope weaseled his way out of custody had vanished.

"When?" Her voice quivered.

"An hour ago. I'm sorry I couldn't warn you sooner. I just found out myself."

Two large blue roller suitcases sat by the front door of her apartment, along with her loaded laptop bag that held her computer and important papers, such as birth certificates and other documents. Lily had dumped her toys on the living room floor and continued to fill a duffel bag with her much-loved stuffed animals. Annie had loaded a couple of storage containers of photos and cherished mementos, as well as a few boxes of household items that included Lily's favorite soft pink comforter, a little while ago. She had the money to replace their things, but ensuring her daughter had her favorites was a necessity—at least for Annie. Lily had lost too much in her short life already. She glanced around the modest two-bedroom apartment she'd moved into when her life had turned upside down the first time, or had it been the second time? Or third? Closing her eyes, she sighed. Everything else was just stuff. But it didn't diminish the hurt of leaving it all behind.

"Annie?"

"Sorry, Doc. We're five minutes from leaving. I only need to load the last little bit." Tears pricked her eyes. The apartment might not be much, but it was her and Lily's home.

"Good. Get out of there. I wish I could have helped you."

"Sir, you've done more than I ever could have asked for."

She'd found a job as a rodeo doctor through a friend of a friend and a small rental house in Rollins, Texas. When she'd told Dr. Gregory she planned to move north, he'd lined up a temporary college-age babysitter. His niece, Karly, loved kids and needed a job for a few weeks before her fall classes began. Annie hadn't wanted anyone to know where she'd moved in case Pope decided to hunt her down, but she couldn't turn down Todd's offer. More than likely he'd discover her location due to Karly.

Once she got settled, she'd apply for a job at the local hospital to fill in her income during the rodeo off-season and find a nanny for Lily. If all worked out, she might consider purchasing her first house. Real estate in small towns tended to be cheaper than in the cities. And she'd saved every penny she could over the years. Thanks to the help of large scholarships and grants, she'd paid off the remaining balance of her school loans and had a sizeable savings due to her modest lifestyle.

"Be safe, Annie." Muffled voices filtered over the line. "I have to go. Please, text me and let me know you made it."

"I will. And thank you."

"You are welcome, my dear. And Annie, I know it doesn't seem like it, but you did the right thing." Dr. Gregory hung up.

She pulled in a deep breath. Time to leave. "Come on, Lily. Let's go on our adventure."

"Okay, Momma." The little girl threw the duffel strap over her shoulder and staggered under the weight. For a four-year-old, it probably felt like a bag of rocks.

Annie took the duffel and handed Lily a roller bag. Her daughter loved to help. And far be it for her to deny the little girl the opportunity. Two trips later, they loaded the last of the items into her midsize SUV.

"Buckle up." She waited for Lily's seat belt to click and shut the door. Annie slid behind the wheel and slipped on her sunglasses. Her eyes went to the rearview mirror. "Ready?"

"Yup." The little girl mimicked her. Lily put on her plastic cat sunglasses and smiled. "Let's go!" She doubted Lily understood what was happening, but her daughter's happiness made the situation easier.

After one last look at the place she'd called home for the past several years, Annie pulled from the parking lot and aimed her SUV north toward the only town that had burrowed deep into her heart. One of safety—she hoped.

After spending the night in a hotel in Lackard, Texas, about forty minutes from her destination, Annie drove the final distance into Rollins the next morning. The larger city gave her an ounce of comfort. Getting lost among people and all that.

Parked in the middle of the rodeo grounds parking lot, she ran her schedule through her mind. Meet with the new babysitter first. Second, she had an appointment with Donovan

Keats about her job in a little over thirty minutes. Then, in the early afternoon, it was off to their new house to unpack and to the store to replace the items they needed. She could do this. Her life had been a series of starting-over moments. What was one more time? *Keep telling yourself that. One day you'll believe it.*

Annie released a long string of air from her lungs. No more pity party. Her mentor, Dr. Gregory, had done her a solid with Karly, and she couldn't thank him enough.

She'd come back to Rollins, Texas, the town of her youth, to escape the devastation in her life. The irony hadn't been lost on her. At thirty years old and one year out of residency, she'd thought her whole life would be ahead of her. A solid reputation and a husband who supported her decisions. But here she sat, running from the threats of a colleague. Annie hadn't had a choice. She'd reported Dr. Layton Pope to the state medical board and the police for stealing narcotics and working impaired during his shifts. Now, she paid the price for doing the right thing. It seemed to be the story of her life.

"Momma, can we get out, please?" The thump of Lily's shoes kicking against the back seat accompanied her daughter's sweet voice.

"Sure, honey." Annie straightened, shot off a quick text to Dr. Gregory that she and Lily had arrived at their destination, and exited her SUV. Lily had more patience than most four-year-olds, but the long drive and the unfamiliar hotel had pushed the girl to the edge of her abilities of sitting still. Since she'd taken custody of her late friend Libby's daughter, Lily, soon after she'd turned one, Annie had grown into the mother role. But the circumstances around the necessity continued to wrap her in guilt.

"Come on, cutie pie. Let's get this party started." She unbuckled the booster seat. Lily launched into Annie's arms and clutched her neck as she lifted the little girl from the vehicle.

"Yay!" Lily kissed her nose.

Annie laughed as the warm humid Texas air enveloped her. She held Lily snug against her and lifted her face to the sun, letting the rays fall on her cheeks. The smell of hay and dust swirled in her nose, making the corner of her lips pull upward. The county fair and rodeo grounds, along with the accompanying carnival, held such wonderful memories from her childhood. It was good to be home after fifteen years.

Lily squirmed. "Down, Momma."

"Sorry." She lowered Lily to the ground. "Stay by my side. There are lots of people and cars."

"Okay." The tiny voice—so trusting. "When's Miss Karly gonna be here? I want to go see the petting zoo."

A smile crossed Annie's face. They'd video chatted with Karly a couple of days ago. The college student and Lily hit it off immediately. Plus, she'd told her daughter about the fair on the way to Rollins. No wonder the little girl was excited. "She'll be here any minute." A blue sedan pulled in next to her SUV. "In fact, that's her right now."

Lily bounced on her toes and squealed.

Dr. Gregory's niece, Karly, strolled over and shook Annie's hand. "Dr. Davis, it's nice to meet you in person."

"Likewise. And please, call me Annie." She placed her hand on Lily's head. "And this is my daughter, Lily."

"Hi, Miss Karly." A huge grin split Lily's face.

Karly crouched to eye level with the four-year-old. "Hi, there. Are you ready to have fun?"

"Yes." Her daughter giggled. "Petting zoo first!"

Annie smiled and shook her head. "I'll let you two get to it. You have my phone number. Text or call if you need anything. Otherwise, I'll touch base after lunch, once I finish my meetings. Feel free to take her to the fair and the carnival. I'll meet up with you in a few hours." She scanned the parking lot.

Karly must have sensed her unease. "Don't worry, Annie. Uncle Todd explained the situation."

Annie's heart skipped a beat. What else had Karly and Todd discussed?

"I'll keep a close eye on her." Karly paused. "And I promise, I've kept your location a secret. Even from my uncle."

She trusted Todd, but the fewer people who could slip up and expose her the better. "Thank you." She knelt and kissed Lily's cheek. "You listen to Karly. Whatever she tells you, you do it without question."

The little girl rolled her eyes. Boy, she would be a handful as a teenager. "I know. I will."

"Good." Annie stood. She handed Karly money for the carnival and treats. "I'll see you two soon."

"Take your time. Come on, Lily, we have animals to pet." The pair took off, hand in hand, their arms swinging in rhythm with each stride.

Annie perused her beloved fairgrounds. A couple of new buildings replaced the old ones, but not much else had changed. The old oak trees stood along the perimeter, leading to the lake on the other side of the wooded area. If the path that meandered from here to the lake could talk, it would speak of innocence and teenage love.

One particular summer fluttered to mind. Daniel's calloused hand entwined with hers. They'd strolled down the shaded path to their favorite spot by the water's edge. Her heart squeezed. Too bad tender moments couldn't be recaptured forever. Daniel, her best friend and first love. She missed him. She'd moved away that school year. Her mother had dragged her to Houston, and Daniel had never given Annie a reason to return to Rollins.

Her gaze drifted to the rodeo arena. Suddenly, she was fifteen, sitting in the stands, watching Daniel clowning around one minute and becoming a serious bullfighter the next. More than once, she'd held her breath when a bull wouldn't relent. But Daniel excelled at his job even at a young age. Warmth spread through her as the memories seeped in.

She glanced at her phone and smiled. Thirty minutes until her meeting with Director Donovan Keats. Enough time to visit the lake and breathe in the fresh air. And maybe for a moment in time, lose herself in the past.

The path meandering through the arch of trees called to her. Her old boots, that she hadn't worn in years, kicked up the parking lot dust. The slight breeze fluttering through the shade cooled the sweat droplets snaking between her shoulder blades as she ambled toward the lake. The quiet was almost earsplitting. Finishing her residency and becoming an instant mom when her best friend died had eliminated quiet moments for the past three years.

The trees parted, revealing the shimmering lake surrounded by woods on three sides. A wave of peace rolled over her. She slowed her steps, drinking in the view. The place hadn't changed since her youth. Sunlight sparkled off the surface. Picnic tables lined the top of the shore, and a generous play and swimming area filled the space between the path and the water's edge.

She smiled at the distant hubbub of the fairgrounds.

The water lapped out of rhythm. Twisting her head to expose her ear to the unusual sound, she narrowed her gaze and listened. Annie straightened and searched for the reason. A man lay half submerged near the shore.

Annie sprinted toward the man, yelling over her shoulder, "Help! Someone, help!" She skidded to a stop and dropped to her knees.

One of the man's arms stretched outward, and the other clutched his side. Blood soaked his shirt. The crimson liquid swirled in the water next to his body.

Annie forced her racing heart to slow and switched to doctor mode. "Sir?" Her fingers pressed against the pulse point on the man's neck. Faint. Thready. But he was alive.

His lids fluttered open. He struggled to focus. A moment later, the man's gaze locked with hers. "Take it," he rasped. He pressed a cool metal object into her hand, then gripped her wrist. The strength of his grasp surprised her. "Follow the evidence." He gasped for air, and his hand fell away.

"I'm a doctor. Help's coming."

His wide eyes darted around the area. "Key…evidence… find…promise."

She'd say almost anything to calm the man down. "I'll take care of it. Try to relax." No idea what she'd promised and why it was important, she shoved the key into her pants pocket. Without a cloth to press against the wound, she used her hand. The blood had slowed but continued to ooze between her fingers. His eyes closed, and his head rolled to the side. If help didn't arrive soon, she'd lose him.

Uncertain anyone had heard her, she fished into her pocket for her cell phone.

Footsteps crunched behind her.

Relief hit her, and she twisted.

A masked man emerged from the trees. A knife glinted in his hand.

Annie's lungs seized. Her patient required pressure on his wound, but she had no choice but to move. Eyes locked on to the masked man, she scrambled away. "Stop!"

No words. No reaction. His boots pounded on the ground as he charged and lunged at her.

She dove to the side a second before the blade sliced through her skin.

Without a weapon in sight, she grabbed a handful of sandy dirt and flung it into his face.

He jerked and stumbled backward. Shaking his head, he swiped his eyes. "You little—" He spit out the sand.

The blood in Annie's ears whooshed from the adrenaline spike. She glanced at the injured man lying in the water. If she didn't escape and get help, they'd both die. Bolting for the path, she stumbled on the uneven shore. A hand grabbed her ankle. She kicked out and connected with the masked man but refused to look back to see where she'd hit him. On all fours, she scrambled up the slight slope. Pebbles pierced her palms. Her heart thundered.

"Help!" The sensation of the man behind her spurred her on. "Please, help." The final plea came out as a whisper.

The unmistakable sound of a woman's scream had sliced through the calm of the afternoon. Daniel tossed his gear, which he'd retrieved moments before, into the bed of his truck and sprinted toward the call for help. Years of work as a deputy had honed his instincts. The scream hadn't come from the joy of the carnival or fairgrounds. The distressed call for help had originated from the lake. His fear of a child in danger urged him on.

He raced down the shaded trail, pushing through dangling vines and limbs. His boot caught the edge of a dip in the ground. He stumbled but kept moving. The pathway opened to the lake.

A tall, lean man in a ski mask closed in on a woman scrambling across the dirt. Strands of unruly hair covered parts of her face, but he didn't miss the terror etching her features.

Daniel poured on speed, wishing he'd retrieved his gun from his truck. "Police!"

The masked man turned a second too slow.

Aiming for his midsection, Daniel hit him at full speed, tackling him to the ground. He grunted at the impact.

A string of curse words pierced the air, and the man tossed him aside.

Daniel had underestimated the guy. That would *not* happen

again. He lifted, ready to defend himself and the woman, when the sun glinted on an ugly-looking knife. The guy swiped at him. Daniel twisted, but the blade caught him on his bicep and slashed his skin. He hissed at the sting of pain. Enough. This had to end now. He slammed his elbow into the attacker's temple.

The knife flew from the man's grip. He fell to the ground and groaned.

Chest heaving, Daniel rolled off the assailant. Hands on his knees, he sucked air into his lungs. He staggered toward the knife that had landed several feet away. Before he could reach it, the masked man rose to his feet, grabbed the weapon, and hurried to the woods.

What had just happened? These days, trouble seemed to follow the carnival and rodeo circuit. Confirming the man had disappeared into the trees, he turned toward the woman—and froze. His heart stopped, then kicked into overdrive. There was no mistaking those eyes or the tiny scar on her left cheekbone from falling out of the hayloft when they were thirteen.

"Annie?" His voice came out hoarse.

Her wide eyes locked on his. "Daniel?"

He hadn't seen her in fifteen years. Not since her mother packed up and left at the beginning of the school year. He and Annie had exchanged a few emails during the first couple of months after she moved to Houston. But it had been crickets the rest of that school year and beyond. He'd checked his inbox daily and spent months wondering why she never wrote back. Then he'd given up, figuring she wanted nothing more to do with him.

But now wasn't the time to dwell on that. Daniel moved to her side and knelt.

"You're bleeding." She eyed his arm.

The gash on his arm stung more than a thousand paper cuts, but he wouldn't bleed out. "I'm fine. Are you hurt?"

She shook her head. “No. But…there’s a man.” She turned and pointed toward the water. “He’s hurt—bad.”

Daniel followed her gaze and spotted the blood-soaked body half in the lake. “Come on.” He helped Annie to her feet and placed a hand on her elbow, steadying her as they rushed to the victim’s side. “What happened?”

“I found him like this. He’s been stabbed.” Her voice, unusually calm for the trauma she’d witnessed and experienced.

Daniel examined the tree line. His brows pulled together. Concern sliced through him. He assumed Annie’s attacker had knifed the man lying in the water, but he had to ask. “Did you see who did this?”

She shook her head. “Just the guy you tackled. I don’t know if he’s the same person who injured this man.” Annie put pressure on the guy’s wound. “He needs an ambulance as soon as possible. He’s lost a lot of blood.”

“I’m on it.” He pulled out his cell phone and called it in.

“Marshall County Dispatch.”

“Regina, this is Deputy Sinclair. I’ve got a critical stabbing victim at the lake behind the fairgrounds. The woman who found the victim was attacked, and the suspect fled the scene after I intervened. Send medical and backup, code three.”

“You got it, Daniel.” He could hear Regina typing. “They’re on the way.”

“Thanks.” He hung up.

Blood continued to seep between Annie’s fingers. “I tried to stop the bleeding earlier, but I don’t have anything to press against the wound except my hand. Then that guy attacked me.”

The injured man’s bloody hand clasped on to Annie’s forearm. “Doc…please.”

“Hang in there. Help is coming.” Annie’s hands pressed harder into the man’s abdomen.

Daniel crouched beside the man. "Sir, do you know who attacked you?"

The man thrashed his head side to side and mumbled something.

Annie leaned in to hear. "Don't worry. I will." She'd say anything to get the man to calm down.

The man went limp.

"I need that ambulance, now!"

"It's on the way." The wail of sirens confirmed his statement. Daniel placed his fingers against his neck. "He has a pulse."

"Not for long if we don't get him to a hospital soon."

He scanned the section of the trees where the attacker had disappeared. He itched to go after the suspect. His gaze drifted to Annie and the injured man and back to the perimeter of the lake.

The ambulance came to a halt. Doors opened and slammed shut. Footfalls pounded on the packed dirt.

Two paramedics, Tanner and Brady, strode toward them, gurney bouncing over the uneven ground, along with Deputy Jackie Bennett and Deputy Vince Wagner.

"What do we have?" Tanner set his medical duffel down and switched places with him.

Annie spoke first. "Victim has a penetrating stab wound to the lower left quadrant of the abdomen, approximately three to four centimeters wide, with moderate to profuse active bleeding. Pulse rapid and thready. Abdomen rigid with guarding—suspected internal bleeding or organ laceration, possibly involving the spleen or intestines. Initiate rapid IV fluids en route. Apply direct pressure to control external bleeding. Expedite immediate transport and alert the Trauma team."

Tanner and Brady exchanged glances and got to work.

"Are you a doctor?" Tanner asked.

"Dr. Annie Davis, emergency medical physician." She

maintained pressure on the wound while the paramedics prepped to take over.

"Good to have you aboard." Brady inserted the IV into the man's arm. "Either of you need immediate medical attention?"

Annie glanced at Daniel's gash then at him and raised an eyebrow.

He shook his head. "I think we're good for now." His cut needed attention, but the stabbing victim was priority.

"Deputy Sinclair, where do you need us?" Jackie's hands rested on her utility belt.

He gave Jackie and Vince the CliffsNotes version of what happened and indicated which way the man had escaped. "One of you cordon off the scene and secure the perimeter. The other put out a search for the man responsible for the attack. It's not much to go on, but it's worth a shot."

"We're on it." Jackie spun, and Vince followed.

Daniel never stopped assessing the woods as he listened to the paramedics and Annie.

"Ready to transport. Dr. Davis, can you maintain pressure?" Brady asked.

"I can, and I will. Get him to the bus."

"Yes, ma'am."

The three moved like they'd worked together for years.

Daniel followed, alert, ready for the masked man to reappear.

With the injured man loaded, Tanner hurried to the driver's side, and Brady hopped in the back of the ambulance. "We've got the patient. Clean up. We'll see you at the hospital." He tossed Daniel a large bottle of water, a roll of gauze, and a towel, then closed the door.

The ambulance left with lights and siren, heading to the local hospital.

During the short time Daniel arrived on scene and the

paramedics whisked their patient away, a small crowd had gathered.

"All right, everyone, the show's over." He flicked his wrist, shooing the onlookers away.

The group slowly dispersed.

He turned to Annie. "Let me help you get cleaned up." He trickled the water over her hands as she rubbed them together then dried them with the towel. "You did good. You kept him alive." He glanced at her fingers, still stained with blood. They both had scrapes and bruises that required tending, and his arm stung like a hundred bee stings, but her shaken expression was what worried him. She looked so unlike the carefree girl he used to know.

"Annie?"

Her brown eyes lifted. "I can't believe it's you."

His heart twisted. "Same. I want to hear more about you and your life, but I hate having you out in the open with that guy on the loose. Plus, we should get to the hospital to check on your patient. Not to mention our own injuries."

She rubbed her hands up and down her arms and flinched when she hit raw skin. "Yes, please. I'll wrap your arm once we're not so exposed."

"We'll take my truck. I'll bring you back when we're done." They both required medical attention. Or at least soap and water and a few Band-Aids.

"I appreciate that." She lowered her gaze as they trekked the path back to the fair and rodeo grounds.

He pointed to his truck. "Over there."

She nodded and followed across the gravel. Once at his vehicle, she used the rest of the water to clean his cut and wound the gauze around his injury. "I need to make a call first, before we go."

"Sure. We'll leave as soon as you're ready." He opened the door for her, and she hopped in.

Placing his own call to his sheriff sister, he updated her on what had happened. When he finished, he circled the vehicle. He hoped he'd given Annie enough time. When he slipped behind the wheel, he noticed the crease between Annie's eyes had deepened. "Problem?"

"My babysitter. The call went in and out. I couldn't really talk to her."

Daniel's lungs seized. Babysitter? She had a kid? He swallowed past the lump in his throat.

She tapped the phone on her chin. "From what I understood, they were at the petting zoo."

"That makes sense. The service can be sketchy in that barn."

The crease in Annie's forehead deepened. "I could hear Lily in the background. It sounded like they were having fun."

"And you're still concerned." Daniel didn't have to ask. Her face spoke of her worries. He examined the park with a trained law enforcement eye. The violence hadn't spilled over from the lake. "Everything seems normal here, but we can go track her down if you want."

"No. You're right. I'm a bit paranoid right now." Her gaze skimmed the area. "Your arm is still bleeding. We need to get you to the hospital and get that stitched up. I'll try again later and hope Karly's in a better spot to have a conversation."

"If you're sure. My arm can wait." Daniel glanced at the blood-soaked gauze. It might make a mess, but it wouldn't kill him.

"Let's take care of that cut. If I can't get through to Karly once that's done, we'll come back and find her."

He started the engine and closed his eyes. Lily. Annie had a kid. Just like that, a decade of unanswered questions flared to life. The news snuffed out any hope to rekindle what they'd once had—assuming she'd want that anyway. Although since she'd ghosted him all those years ago, probably not.

Before he dug into the past, he needed answers as to what happened at the lake.

If the attacker discovered the injured man had talked to Annie, Daniel had no doubt the man would be back to finish the job.

TWO

Annie hated that the call to Karly had glitched. The conversation might have been in bits and pieces, but at least her babysitter had picked up. She hesitated to leave the rodeo grounds without putting eyes on her daughter, but the attack hadn't appeared to affect the fairgrounds or the carnival. She shouldn't be worried, but…hello… The mother in her said otherwise.

The clock on her phone indicated that her appointment time with Keats had come and gone. What a way to make an impression, but the emergency demanded her attention. She tapped out a text to the rodeo director, informing him that she'd meet with him once she returned from the hospital and gave her statement to the deputies. And hugging her daughter, but he didn't need to know that, so she left that part off.

Scraping her teeth on her bottom lip, she stared out the passenger window. Under normal circumstances, Annie would've embraced the drive through town, but today—not so much—especially with the man sitting beside her.

"So, you're a doctor, huh?" Daniel tapped his thumbs on the steering wheel.

Annie shifted to face him. "An emergency medical physician. I spent the last few years working in a high-volume San Antonio emergency department."

"And you're here to work at Rollins General Hospital?"

"Nope. I got the job of the resident rodeo doctor."

The truck jerked to the right, then straightened. Daniel coughed. "You're Dr. Anderson Davis?"

She cocked her head and studied him. "Yes, but I've always gone by Annie. Anderson is a family name."

His shoulder shook until he couldn't hold it in any longer. A deep belly laugh filled the cab.

Well, now, didn't that just hurt? "My name's not funny."

When he got himself under control, he wiped his eyes. "No. No, it's not. Sorry."

"Then why are you laughing at me?"

"I'm not. I'm cracking up because the guys are going to get the shock of their lives."

"Not a fan of women doctors?" She hadn't thought it would be a big deal, but apparently, she'd made a mistake.

"They'll be fine. No one will disrespect you. I promise. But when you're expecting a man, and a woman shows up…" He chuckled. "I can't wait to see their faces."

She crossed her arms. The last thing she needed was more drama surrounding her career.

He glanced in her direction. "I'm sorry. I didn't mean to hurt your feelings. And no, the guys won't have an issue once they digest the information."

"Are you sure?" Keats had assured her that the cowboys and cowgirls would respect her, but now she wasn't so confident.

"Positive. Please, trust me."

How could she not? The boy she remembered had never let her down. Well, until he cut all ties to her. But lie? No. He'd never done that except for not responding to her emails. "I'm going to take your word for that." She glanced at her phone, resisting the urge to call Karly again.

"So, you have a kid?" Daniel's question yanked her from her thoughts.

"Yes. And no."

He did a double take. "I think you need to explain that."

She would have laughed at his expression if the current situation wasn't so serious and Lily's past wasn't heartbreaking.

"I have a daughter. She's four, and her name is Lily."

"And your husband? Her father?"

"It's not like that. I never married. Lily is adopted. Her mother, Libby, my best friend through college, and her husband died a few days after Lily turned one." Annie's heart twisted. If only she could've saved her friend. She swallowed—hard. "I promised to raise Lily if anything happened to them." She spread her hands. "Well, it happened. Presto. Mom. Not an easy thing to do during residency."

"I can imagine." Daniel's cheeks puffed, and he exhaled. "Boyfriend?"

She laughed, but there was no humor behind it. "That's a story for another occasion. But no."

She noticed his eyes scanning the mirrors.

Twisting in her seat, she searched the road and the landscape. "Did you see something?"

"No. Just staying alert."

"Okay. That's good." She rubbed along the edge of the scrapes on her hand.

The hospital came into view several blocks ahead. The small building she remembered now had additional wings.

"Wow, they added on since I moved away."

Daniel nodded. "We're a central location in the county. The town and county teamed together to make it the central hub for Marshall County."

"Makes sense." After giving the rodeo doc thing some time, she'd see if they had any openings and apply here to work part-time at the hospital as well.

Daniel parked the car. "Let's check on our injured man and get ourselves cleaned up. Izzie should be here soon."

"Izzie? Why would your sister come?"

"She's the Marshall County sheriff. And pretty good at it, but don't tell her I said so."

Annie flipped her gaze to him. The smirk told her all she needed to know. "Still Mr. Funny Man?"

"Meh. I try." The cheesy grin told her he not only tried but succeeded. Strange. The idea he hadn't changed comforted her. "Come on."

She slipped from the truck and groaned. Her muscles had tightened, and standing straight sent an ache through her that had her mentally begging for a massage.

They strode in silence through the emergency department entrance. Daniel headed to the receptionist.

He tapped his fist on the desk. "Hey, Aunt Rachel."

If Annie remembered correctly, the older lady was his mom's best friend and honorary family member.

"Hey, yourself." She looked him over. Her perusal halted on the bandage Annie had wrapped around the cut on his bicep. "I don't know why you're here, but you *will* see a doctor before you leave."

He shrugged. "It's only a scratch."

The older woman snorted. "Right. And I'm twenty-one."

"Not a day over." Daniel grinned.

Boy, the man *hadn't* changed. Always good for a joke or to lighten the mood.

Rachel swatted at him. "Oh, you. What can I do for you?"

Daniel leaned against the desk and crossed his ankles. "The stabbing victim who arrived a little while ago, we need info on him."

"Your sister is back with him now."

"How'd Izzie get here so fast?"

"Don't look at me." The woman shrugged.

"Thank you, Miss Rachel." Annie smiled.

The Sinclairs' honorary aunt's eyes widened. "Oh my! Is that you, Annie Davis?"

"Yes, ma'am."

"It's good to see you again." Rachel's eyes darted between Annie and Daniel. A smirk tugged on the woman's lips. She waved them toward the chairs. "Have a seat. Daniel, I'll tell that sheriff sister of yours that you're out here. After that, I'll grab a doctor to clean you two up."

"Thanks, Aunt Rachel." He held his hand out, gesturing for Annie to go before him.

She maneuvered around a few chairs and headed to the corner on the far side of the waiting room. The emergency department in Rollins felt like a deserted town. Nothing like the hospital she left a couple of days ago. Had it really only been yesterday that she and Lily packed up and hurried from the city?

"Hopefully, Izzie will have a few answers for us." He dropped onto the chair next to her.

The white bandage she put on his arm had turned red. "Rachel's right. That cut needs attention."

"And I'll have it taken care of. But first, I want to know who that man is. Second, is the why of it."

Annie checked her phone. She sighed. "After everything that's happened, I can't stand it. I'm going to call Karly again." The call went to voicemail. She left a message and tapped End. "I don't understand why Karly isn't answering."

"The fairgrounds and carnival are noisy. She might not hear it. And if she's in the barns, those bleating sheep and goats will make your ears bleed with all that racket."

She puffed out a breath. "You have a point. I did talk with her earlier—kinda. I'll try texting in a bit."

"I had a text awaiting me from Izzie when we arrived. She said today's lake events hadn't bled over to the rest of the area. Plus, she's beefed up security. She just hadn't said she was already here."

"That's good to know." Annie had been protective of Lily

since the day she'd picked her up after Libby's death. Now, if she could convince herself that Karly would put Lily's safety first if something happened it would ease her nerves.

Izzie pushed open the hallway double doors and strode to the waiting room.

She and Daniel moved to meet his sister.

"Daniel." Izzie's gaze moved to her. "Annie!" A smile bloomed on her face. Izzie enveloped her in a hug. "It's good to see you."

"I'd like to say it's good to be back in Rollins, but..." She pointed in the direction Izzie had come from.

"Well, I can understand that." Daniel's sister motioned to the chairs they'd vacated. "Have a seat. I'll tell you what I know. Then, the two of you will get medical help."

Annie sat and clasped her hands on her lap.

"I've heard from my other deputies. They haven't found the man responsible for the attack. However, the fairgrounds and carnival appear to be secure. I talked with Keats. Between my deputies and the hired security, we've doubled the eyes on the park. I want your official statements as soon as we take care of business here." Izzie sighed. "I've got the gist of what happened to you and the guy lying on the hospital bed back there. But I want the full story."

"Do you know who he is?" Annie hated that he was a nameless victim.

Izzie leaned in and lowered her voice. "The guy's an undercover deputy from Lonehart County, two counties over. He's working as a carnie trying to track down where the influx of fentanyl is coming from."

Daniel matched his sister's stance and added a conspiratorial tone. "Well, sis, I think the dude's cover is blown. If not, he flat out made someone mad." Daniel pursed his lips together, raised his brows, and shrugged.

"Ya think?" Izzie rolled her eyes. "Why do I put up with you?"

"Because you love me." He waggled his eyebrows.

"Bro, for once, be serious."

"Serious is boring." Daniel flicked his hand. "Go on."

Annie ran her gaze over him. He'd always loved to have fun, and true, she hadn't seen him in over a decade, but there was something below his antics. Maybe. Okay, so she might be reaching, but she didn't think so.

"As I was saying…the deputy's name is Gordon Bonner. I called the Lonehart County sheriff. He's rounding up the latest reports. He'll send them as soon as he talks to the deputy's handler." Izzie's eyes drifted from Daniel to her. "Annie, if you hadn't acted, Bonner wouldn't have made it this far."

She nodded, but the physician in her knew the probability of the man surviving. "When are they taking him into surgery?"

"They're giving him blood and waiting on the trauma surgeon to get here from Lackard." Izzie checked her watch. "I'd say within the next thirty minutes."

"I'm not sure that will be quick enough. But without the transfusion, he won't make it anyway."

"That's what the doc said, but he's hopeful. This isn't the first time we wished we had a trauma doctor on-site."

An idea popped into Annie's head. But it would have to wait until later.

Izzie blew out a breath. "We can't do anything without the file from Lonehart County or without talking to Deputy Bonner about his role in this. Why don't the two of you see to your injuries? I'll maintain a presence out here, and now that I know what's going on with Bonner, I'll call in a deputy to stand guard outside his door." The sheriff pointed to Daniel's arm. "Looks like you need patching up."

He shrugged and winced. "It could use a couple of stitches."

Annie's eyes shot open wide. "Did he admit he needs medical help?"

"I do believe he did." Izzie nodded.

Daniel glared at both of them.

Izzie laughed and stood. "I'll grab a nurse."

A few minutes later, Nurse Tina escorted them to separate emergency bays.

"I don't like you out of my sight," Daniel protested, but Tina gave him a gentle shove into the small exam room.

"I'll be fine," Annie called after him. She entered the other room, sat on the bed, and closed her eyes. What had she gotten herself into? Why couldn't she have a normal peaceful life for once?

Tina returned a few minutes later, cleaned her wounds, and bandaged the severest of the scrapes. "Deputy Sinclair will be a bit longer. I'd offer you to stay here, but we have a patient who arrived in the waiting room, and we only have a few beds."

The downside of a small-town hospital. Or, maybe it was an upside. "Not a problem. I'll go peek in on my patient."

Tina raised a single eyebrow.

"You know I'm a doctor, and I'm the one who treated him in the field. I promise not to step on any toes."

The nurse smiled. "The trauma doc from Lackard should be here any minute. Make it quick."

"Thank you." Annie eased off the bed and wandered to Deputy Bonner's bay at the end of the hall, skirting a cart parked in the middle of the walkway. Tina hadn't been kidding about the size of the emergency department here. Four bays along one wall.

She eased the door open, stepped inside, and jolted to a halt.

A man in a medical mask loomed over Deputy Bonner, syringe in hand.

"What are you doing?"

The guy looked up and lunged forward, aiming the needle at her.

Annie spun to escape. Hands grabbed her hair and yanked. She stumbled, landing on the floor—hard. She crab walked backward.

The man stalked toward her with the syringe fisted and held high. The glint in his eye—evil, pure evil.

"Please, don't." Her voice cracked, and her heart slammed against her ribs. She had no idea what the syringe contained, but it couldn't be good.

The mask hid most of her attacker's face, but the skin on the sides of his eyes crinkled. The jerk was smiling.

He sprang forward.

Annie brought her knees to her chest and shot her legs out. Her feet caught the masked man in the torso, knocking him off balance and into the roller hospital tray. The table crashed to the floor.

Searching for anything she could use for a weapon, Annie scrambled to her feet and plastered her back to the wall. What would happen to Lily if this guy succeeded in killing her?

Pulling in a breath, she found her voice. "Help!"

"Help me!"

The terror in Annie's scream launched Daniel off the exam table. He tore out of the room—the suture thread dangling from his upper arm. He bolted into the corridor, ignoring the blood trickling from his bicep to his elbow. The doc hadn't finished, but it didn't matter. Annie's call for help had sent icy fingers crawling up his spine, gripping the base of his skull.

Daniel skirted the cart sitting in the hall and flung open the door to the next room where Annie had gone. Nothing. A ruckus farther down grabbed his attention. He sprinted to the bay at the end of the short hallway. His heart pounded so hard he thought it might bust a rib. He rushed in and skidded to a halt.

Annie's wide terrified eyes gutted him. His gaze jerked to the assailant.

The guy staggered to his feet and stalked toward her. He clocked the man at around six feet tall with what looked like brown hair sticking out beneath a scrub cap.

"Police!" Daniel didn't have a weapon but refused to let that stop him.

The stranger whirled and barreled into him like a two-thousand-pound bull. Daniel's back slammed into the floor. Air whooshed from his lungs and pain radiated through his shoulder as his head skimmed the tile. The attacker pushed up, pinballed off the wall, and stumbled out of the door.

Struggling to suck in precious oxygen, Daniel clutched the end of the bed and hoisted himself to a standing position. "Annie?"

She flipped her hair from her face. "I'm okay. Go!"

He took off after the assailant. Hand on the door frame, he flung himself out of the room into the hallway.

"Izzie!" Daniel prayed his sister heard him through the closed doors to the waiting room.

The guy who'd attempted to hurt Annie hit the crash bar on the emergency exit. Sunlight spilled in as the man escaped outside.

His sister pushed open the doors and sprinted toward him. "What's wrong?"

Daniel wrapped an arm around his middle, putting supportive pressure on his sore ribs, and pointed. "Male, approximately six feet with possible brown hair, attacked Annie."

"On it." Izzie called dispatch and relayed the information. "Take care of Annie," his sister called over her shoulder as she hurried out the door to hunt the guy down.

Pain radiated up his back and around his torso. Nothing

serious. Remnants of being tackled and hitting the hard floor. He glanced down. Tiny blood droplets splattered the floor like confetti. At least it didn't look like a scene from a horror flick.

The black suture thread stuck to his arm. The doc had had a couple of stitches left when Daniel rushed out of the room. Blood continued to drip from his elbow, caused by physical exertion. Guess he'd have to finish up the stitches once he checked on Annie.

He entered the room where he'd left her. He stopped next to the bed. "He disappeared out the emergency exit."

She straightened from where she leaned over, examining the undercover deputy, and pointed to the floor. "Collect that syringe for evidence and get it to the lab. Be careful. I have no idea what's in it."

Tissue in hand, he picked up the offending object seconds before the room erupted into chaos.

The doctor and nurses surrounded the officer and frantically checked Bonner over.

Arms wrapped around her middle, Annie moved aside, allowing the hospital personnel to do their jobs.

Daniel heard comments about the trauma surgeon arriving and prepping the deputy for surgery. He guided her into the hall, out of the way of the medical team. He ignored the residual ache in his body, focusing instead on her pale face. "Talk to me, Annie."

Her voice quivered. "He tried to inject something into Deputy Bonner's IV."

Daniel glanced at the room they'd vacated. The man hadn't targeted Annie. Bonner had been the guy's focus. His gut twisted. "Did the attacker get to him?"

"No." Annie rubbed her arms as if chilled despite the warmth in the room. "I startled him. We struggled. He came at me, and I kicked him into the roller table. The next thing I knew, you charged through the doorway."

Daniel lifted the syringe and eyed the clear liquid. "We need to get this tested."

The emergency bay door swung open. He and Annie scooted out of the way, and the medical staff rolled Deputy Bonner toward the surgery wing.

Boots clomped on the hospital floor. Izzie strode toward them, her face tight with frustration. "He vanished. The guy must've had a car waiting."

"Figures."

"What's that?" His sister pointed at the syringe.

"I don't know what's in it, but according to Annie, the guy tried to inject it into Bonner's IV. When she stopped him, he came after her with it."

"I'll take it. The field test kit is back at the office. We'll have to wait to see if we can get a positive on the drug."

Daniel handed her the syringe, which she placed in a plastic container. "We need extra eyes on Bonner and Annie other than hospital security while I finish getting this thing stitched." He lifted his blood-smeared arm.

"Deputy Carpenter arrived a few minutes ago. I sent him to the surgical suite to protect Bonner. I'll keep Annie company until you finish up." Izzie's eyes softened as she turned to Annie. "Are you sure you're okay?"

"I'm fine." Annie stared at her phone. "After everything that's happened, I just want to hold my daughter in my arms."

Izzie's gaze jerked to Annie's. "You have a daughter?"

Daniel held up a hand. "Izz, it's a bit of a story. Can we not go there right now?"

"Yeah, sure. It just surprised me, that's all."

"Let's wrap things up here and get to the station so she can get back to her daughter." Daniel turned to Annie. "Since Deputy Bennett and Wagner are at the rodeo grounds, we'll ask them to locate Lily and Karly, get eyes on her, and take a picture to ease your momma heart."

"Send Daniel and me a picture of Lily, and Karly if you have one." Izzie rattled off her phone number and added Daniel's as well.

"I hate to have you go to that trouble, but I really appreciate it." Annie typed in the information and included a photo of Lily in the group text. "I don't have one of Karly. We just got to town. She's my friend's niece."

"Lily's picture should be enough to find them." Izzie got to work informing the other deputies.

"Marshall County Sheriff's Department has a good crew." Daniel's heart shattered at the strain in Annie's features. "They'll find Lily so you can visibly see she's okay. I promise." Wow. Had he really just said that? He knew better, especially after his experiences in law enforcement.

Annie's fingers wrapped around his good arm. "I know you can't make that promise. As an emergency department doctor, I live in the real world. A world where tragedies happen. But I appreciate the sentiment. And thank you for going the extra mile to alleviate my fears."

The woman had grit. He'd give her that. "Let's get you settled, and I'll take care of this scratch." He escorted her to the waiting room.

"Scratch, huh?"

"Well, maybe a claw mark." More like a groove the size of Texas that stung like a scorpion strike, but he wouldn't admit it.

"I can see things haven't changed." Annie lowered onto a chair.

He lifted a shoulder and plastered a smile on his face. "What can I say? I'm fun." Except he didn't feel like Mr. Happy right now. He struggled to maintain the carefree attitude everyone expected of him. He walked away, trusting his sister to protect Annie.

Ten minutes later, Daniel sat in the emergency bay and

managed to stay still long enough for the doctor to finish suturing his arm.

The doctor snipped the thread and placed the equipment onto the metal tray. "Deputy Sinclair, next time, try to avoid the knife. You know the drill. Keep it dry for a few days." The man snapped his gloves off and tossed them in the trash. "I'll have Tina bring you the after-care instructions. But you have enough of them to wallpaper an entire wall, so I'm sure you know what to do."

"Funny, Doc. Very funny." He thanked the doctor, and once Tina gave him the instructions, he strolled to the waiting room.

Annie sat next to Izzie, studying her phone, almost as if willing it to ring.

He joined them, flexing his fingers. The muscles ached and the skin pulled, but the local anesthetic hadn't worn off, so the pain was minimal. For now. He chuffed. It was going to hurt like a big dog when the feeling returned. "All done."

Annie glanced at the white bandage that wrapped his arm, lifted her gaze to him, and nodded. "Glad to see the doctor was able to finish."

"I can be good."

Izzie snorted.

"What?" His impersonation of innocence made Annie laugh. That, right there, was worth the effort. "Meet ya at the office, Izz."

"You got it. Take over the conference room."

He nodded and escorted Annie to his truck.

Tense silence filled the cab on the short drive to the sheriff's station. Annie's repeated attempts to contact Karly had gone unanswered.

"Still nothing?" He glanced at her and back to the road.

"I've heard from her through a couple of text messages a little while ago. She said Lily is having a great time." She held the phone in both hands and tapped it on her thigh. "Maybe it's just me who needs the comfort of my daughter."

"Let me ask you this. Would you be concerned if you hadn't been attacked at the lake?"

Her brow furrowed. She blinked several times. "No. I don't think so. I'm just being overly sensitive right now."

"Understandable. We can go check real quick if you want."

"No. The deputies are looking for them to ease my nerves, and I've heard from Karly. Let's go to the station and take care of business."

"If you're sure."

"I am." She sighed. "When did I become *that mother*? The one who didn't want her child out of her sight—ever. It's funny. I used to look at others and shake my head at their overprotectiveness. Man, was I wrong."

"That's a pretty common assumption." Annie's unsettled vibe had Daniel questioning his thoughts. His focus had centered on Annie this whole time, but now…

He blew out a long slow breath, easing his roiling stomach. Children, especially those missing and hurt, were his kryptonite. An incident years ago at the sheriff's academy where a little boy died because he couldn't reach the child in time had left him gun-shy around kids.

He hadn't met Lily, but it didn't matter. The fears traveling through him were the same. He had no reason to think the worst. Annie had communicated with Karly. But still…

Please, God, don't let me make a mistake about Lily's safety.

THREE

"No answer?"

After they arrived at the sheriff's office, unease had settled in Annie's belly, and she couldn't shake it. She ended the call and placed her phone on the conference room table. She lifted her gaze to Daniel. Unable to find her voice, she shook her head. Her hands trembled. Bile rose in her throat from the fear twisting her stomach. The air conditioner kicked on, and the cool breeze from the vents sent a shiver down her back. The off-white walls and drab chair color resembled her mood. The bright painting of downtown Rollins hanging on the opposite side of the room had a jarring cheerfulness.

Daniel rested his hand over hers. "Izzie's checking with Jackie and Vince for an update."

"Who?" Her neurons refused to fire. She'd thought escaping Dr. Pope's threats had ranked highest on her stress meter. Boy, had she been wrong. Not with the guy who'd attacked her at the lake. However, if it hadn't been for the undercover deputy, she'd have thought Pope had found her and made good on his promise to hurt her and Lily.

"Deputy Bennett and Deputy Wagner."

"I remember now. Sorry." The broken call and text messages had relieved the persistent worry. Only her mother desire to hold her child remained—until now. A switch had flipped.

Deep down in her gut, she had a bad feeling about the babysitter and her daughter. She wanted nothing more than to rush to the fairgrounds and tear the place upside down. But why? Because Karly hadn't answered her call? There were a thousand reasons for that.

"No need to be sorry." He squeezed her hand.

"I'm really worried." She swallowed past the lump in her throat. She couldn't shake the black cloud of concern.

"Never discount your instinct. But don't overreact either." Daniel's brow furrowed. "You just moved back, correct?"

"Yes. Lily and I spent the night in Lackard and drove in this morning."

He scratched at the stubble along his jawline. The rasp barely registered over her pounding heart. "How well do you know Karly?"

Annie's head swung side to side. "No. You don't understand. Karly's uncle—he helped me with a bad situation. I trust him with my life—and Lily's."

Daniel's expression softened. "All right. I'm sorry. I didn't mean to upset you. I'm only trying to figure out if there's a real cause for worry."

Izzie strode in and dropped onto an office chair at the conference table. "Since Jackie and Vince were at the carnival, they searched there first then looped over to the rodeo grounds as soon as we called. They're headed to the fairgrounds next. There's no sign of Lily or Karly, and you know how iffy the service can be in certain barns over there. Plus, the carnival is noisy. Not a great place to hear a phone ring. I'm not discounting your instincts, but as of now, there's nothing to suggest foul play. I recommend we get the statements completed and questions asked and answered. Then, we'll join the search if my deputies haven't found the pair."

What could she say? The sheriff needed the reports to protect the community and find the person responsible for stabbing Deputy Bonner and attacking her and Daniel. As for Lily being in danger, she had nothing more than a recent unanswered call and a sour stomach.

Izzie shifted into sheriff mode. "Let's get through this as quickly as possible so we can get you to the park. Normally, I'd question the two of you separately, but my deputy—" she pinned a glare at her brother "—knows better than to interrupt."

Daniel placed a hand over his chest. "I'm wounded."

"Right. Well, you and your wound can stay quiet." Izzie shook her head. "You'll have to excuse him."

Memories tugged a sad smile from Annie. She remembered the fun-loving quality in her old friend, but the humor no longer made it to his expressive eyes, as if something or someone had extinguished the pure joy the man used to display even when life turned hard with his father's betrayal. Or maybe she'd imagined it. It wasn't like Annie's brain was firing on all cylinders after two attacks and not being able to see Lily in person.

Izzie leaned forward. "Tell me what happened, then I'll have you write it down while I grill my brother."

Daniel snorted. "Whatever. I'll write my statement out now. That way, we can head to the rodeo grounds when I finish the debrief."

"Perfect." Izzie handed him a pen and paper, then shifted her gaze to Annie. "Start when you arrived in town. It'll help you organize your thoughts."

She disagreed, but Izzie spoke the truth about the chaos rattling around in her mind. "I have a new job here in Rollins. Lily and I left San Antonio yesterday and spent the night in Lackard…"

The retelling of the events brought back the man's attack in full color detail. Her head swam, and her body shook. If it hadn't been for Daniel on two different occasions, she'd be dead.

He clutched her fingers. "Hey, you're okay. I'll protect you. And Izzie's the best at finding bad guys." The same quirky smile she remembered lifted the corner of his mouth.

"Thank you."

Daniel shifted the pen and paper to her. "Write down what you saw and did from the moment you discovered Deputy Bonner until we left the hospital, then sign and date the bottom."

She nodded. Daniel leaned back in his chair and clasped his hands over his stomach. His words swirled in the air just out of reach of Annie's mind as he filled Izzie in on his part of the story.

Annie clutched the pen tighter, forcing herself to focus on her statement. Her hand trembled as she wrote. Her vision blurred at the edges. How would she live with the guilt and pain if something happened to Lily?

Daniel squeezed her shoulder.

She glanced around the room. "Are you finished?"

He tilted his head, studying her. "Yes. Izzie went to take care of a few things."

When had he stopped talking? Her whirling thoughts that she couldn't corral were disturbing. "I know we have to do this, and you guys are hurrying, but I have to talk to Lily." Eyes locked on to her hands, Annie gave a sad chuckle. "She's probably having the time of her life."

"Probably. We'll leave in a few minutes, after you finish. Then we'll locate her and ease your fears. Hang in there."

She lifted her gaze to meet his. His steadiness offered an anchor to her spiraling dread.

"She's just a little girl." Annie's voice cracked. "If anything has happened—"

"Don't go there. Bad cell service happens a lot at the fairgrounds. Besides, there's a lot to occupy their time."

Annie wanted to believe him. She *needed* to believe him.

"What time were you supposed to meet up with Karly?"

"I'd scheduled her for the day, but I planned to meet them after lunch at around two."

"Well, there ya go. It's not two yet. Karly will find a place to check her phone and see you've called then."

"You think?" She wanted to grasp on to the hope, but the niggling doubt in her head refused to let her.

Daniel shrugged. "All I'm saying is, don't panic until we have something to worry about."

"That's harder to do once you become a parent."

Before he responded, Izzie returned to the conference room. Tension etched her features.

Lily. Annie stiffened, her pulse roaring in her ears.

Daniel sat up straight. "What's wrong?"

Izzie's gaze darted between them. "Bonner didn't make it. He died on the operating table."

The words hit Annie like a physical blow. She sucked in a shuddering breath, guilt and helplessness crashing down on her. Similar to the night Libby died. "I should've done more."

Daniel shook his head. "You did everything you could."

"Why did the guy stab him? Had Bonner's cover been blown?" she asked.

"That's what we'll try to figure out. I called his boss and delivered the news, along with requesting to speak directly with his handler and get as much information about his case as possible since it landed in my county." Izzie leaned against the wall, looking exhausted for the middle of the day. "The only thing that makes sense beyond a random mugging is that he discovered evidence that got him killed."

Annie pressed a fist against her chest, trying to ease the ache. Losing a patient had never become routine for her. Daniel was right, she'd worked hard to keep Bonner alive—and now he was gone. Izzie's assumption made sense.

Pen gripped tight, she refocused on the paper in front of her. Wait. Evidence. The key.

She dug into her pocket, pulled out the metal key, and held it out. "I completely forgot about this. Bonner gave it to me before he lost consciousness. He told me to follow the evidence."

Izzie took the key from her, examined it, and handed it to Daniel. "Did he say anything else?"

Annie nodded. "He said not to trust anyone. But I can't do this alone, and I trust the two of you. I have no idea what it unlocks. He didn't say, or not that I understood."

Daniel stared at it before wrapping his fingers around it and making a fist. "It might be to a locker or a deposit box. I think you're right, Izzie. Whatever Bonner found got him killed."

Annie's stomach churned as she finished her statement and handed it to Izzie. How much danger were they in—and what had Bonner trusted her to protect?

"One more thing before we head out." Izzie had brought a few small field test kits with her when she returned. She set them on the table and pulled out the syringe Daniel had recovered. She slipped on gloves. "I'm working a hunch. Since Bonner's case focused on fentanyl, I'm testing for that first. The real test will be done in the lab, but this will tell us what we need to know."

Annie watched Izzie drop a small liquid sample into the test pouch and shake it hard, releasing the reagent. Within seconds, the solution turned a vivid orange.

"Fentanyl." Izzie blew out a puff of air. She pointed to the syringe. "That much would've killed you or Bonner if the attacker had succeeded."

In the past several hours, Annie's life had turned upside down. She worried about Dr. Layton Pope's threat but never expected to be thrown into this nightmare. Annie gripped the edge of the desk. The room tilted for a moment. "Can we please go find Lily?"

"We're done here. I'll file your statements and contact you if I have more questions."

"You know where to find me." Annie had told Izzie about her job as the rodeo doctor and had given the sheriff her new address for the three-bedroom rental house in the middle of town.

An older lady hurried in and handed Izzie a slip of paper.

"Thanks, Cory."

"Sure thing, Sheriff." The woman exited the room.

Izzie read the note. "Dispatch received a call. A college-aged girl OD'd at the fairgrounds."

Annie's heartbeat stuttered. Could it be Karly? What had Annie exposed Lily to? She had come to Rollins to escape a threat, not place her and her daughter in more danger. "Did they find a little girl?"

"Not that they reported. Just the young woman." Izzie's empathetic tone brought tears to Annie's eyes.

Daniel exchanged a quick look with Izzie and nodded. "Let's head out there."

"Yes, please." Too much had happened, and until Annie had Lily in her arms, she wouldn't relax. She hated the black storm cloud hovering over her favorite place growing up. But more than that, she prayed the gnawing alarm in her stomach would dissipate.

The silent drive from the sheriff's office to the park that contained the carnival, rodeo, and fairgrounds spiked Daniel's nerves. He hated the quiet. It allowed too much time to think. He tamped down the desire to make a joke. A go-to he'd perfected. Was he a happy guy? The majority of the time—yes. But his jokester self had taken on a life of its own. First, when his mom kicked his father out after he'd had an affair.

Who was Daniel kidding? Multiple affairs. Then, when tragedy with the child struck during the sheriff's academy, it had become his shield. No one knew about his nightmares. About the screams in his head that wouldn't die. His stomach flip-flopped at the memories. Would the anxiety ever leave him?

Daniel followed Izzie's sheriff SUV into the fairground parking lot and maneuvered his vehicle to the rear unused dirt lot with overgrown weeds.

The flashing red-and-blue lights bounced off the back of the cattle barn. He'd silently questioned if the deceased could be Karly but hadn't wanted to voice the possibility and scare Annie. But a gut-deep dread clawed at his chest.

"Do you think it's Karly?" Annie choked out the question he'd feared to voice.

"I won't lie to you." He couldn't. Not with his childhood best friend. His first love. The girl—now woman—who'd set the standard for what he wanted in a relationship. "It crossed my mind. As of right now, there's no news of a little girl. Before we speculate any further, let's get the facts."

Annie nodded. "I can work with facts." As a doctor, he had no doubts she spoke the truth.

He put the truck into Park and killed the engine. "Stick with me, or they won't let you beyond the barrier."

"Got it." Annie opened her door and slid from the truck. Her pallor bothered him, but she appeared to have shaken off the lingering effects from the attack and news about Bonner.

He watched her, wondering about her life over the past ten-plus years. Daniel pushed aside his curiosity and exited the vehicle.

Izzie met them at the front of the truck. "Time to find out what's going on."

Hand on the small of Annie's back—not to guide her, but to give her a measure of comfort—he followed his sister to the crime scene tape draped along rusty metal poles still standing from bygone years.

"Sheriff Sinclair. Deputy Sinclair." The department's newest deputy, Aiden Lane, greeted them. Izzie had legally changed her name to Sinclair-Russell after she married Logan but continued to use Sinclair for her job as sheriff for simplicity's sake.

Daniel scanned the cordoned-off area. Nothing odd stood out. His gaze landed on the body. The county coroner crouched, examining the girl. How had Dr. Joel Vance beaten them to the scene?

Izzie stood feet apart, resting her hands on her hips. "Deputy, has the woman been identified yet?"

"No, ma'am."

"Anything else I need to be aware of?"

"Yes, ma'am. The coroner arrived a few minutes ago, and Deputy Wagner is still searching for the child as per your request."

"Were the paramedics called?"

Deputy Lane shook his head. "A Mr. Conor Murray found the deceased. He said he called out for help and checked for a pulse. He found none. Deputy Bennett was nearby and responded. Bennett confirmed Mr. Murray's assessment and called the coroner."

"Thanks, Deputy." Izzie shifted to face Daniel. "Shall we see what the good doctor has discovered?"

Daniel let the rhetorical question slide and held the ribbon up, motioning for Annie and Izzie to duck under.

Deputy Bennett waved them over.

The humidity-filled air mixed with dust and the odor of cattle. Daniel wiped the sweat from his brow. Welcome to Texas in the summer.

A small form lay near the old abandoned loading chute behind the barn, curled onto her side, facing away from the small crowd that had formed. A petite brunette, from what he could tell. He moved Annie to the other side for a full view of the girl.

Annie's breath caught.

Gravel and hay tangled in the girl's long dark hair. One of her shoes was missing. "Is it Karly?" He kept his voice low so others beyond their little group couldn't hear.

Covering her mouth, Annie nodded.

Izzie's eyes met his. Her chin dipped in acknowledgment.

Annie's spine straightened. Her eyes darted along the edge of the overgrown section of the fairgrounds—no doubt searching for Lily. But the woman's resolve stood strong.

Once they had information about Karly's death, he'd pull together a search party and find Annie's little girl. He fought the urge to pull her into a hug. Time had passed, and he no longer held that right.

"Hey, Doc. What do you have?" Izzie stood next to Dr. Vance.

"Just got here, so I haven't done a full evaluation, but judging from the temperature of the body and the beginning onset of rigor mortis the young woman probably died forty-five minutes to an hour ago. Based on first look, I'd say Deputy Bennett called it correctly." He pointed to the dried foam around Karly's mouth and lifted her arm, exposing the inside of her elbow. "An overdose."

Annie surprised Daniel and crouched next to the coroner. She visually examined Karly's body. "I've seen tons of overdose emergencies in the ER. They don't look like this. The injection site—it's too clean, too high, too deep." She turned her head toward Izzie, who now stood beside Daniel with a frontal view of Karly. "This wasn't self-inflicted unless she was hallucinating before the fatal dose. And I'd stake my medical license on the fact she wasn't high when I met with her this morning."

"Doc?" Daniel respected the coroner enough to ask him to confirm Annie's conclusion.

Dr. Vance's brow furrowed as he leaned closer and trailed a gloved finger over the injection sight. His head slowly bobbed up and down. "She's right." His gaze met Annie's. "Dr. Joel Vance, local coroner and family physician in these parts. It's nice to meet you."

"Dr. Annie Davis, emergency medical physician and new rodeo doctor. And likewise." Lips pressed together, she stood and ran her hands up and down her arms. Her gaze swept the scene like a trained investigator.

Daniel joined in the scan of the surrounding area. "Izz, Karly's phone's not here. Annie, did she have a purse?"

"A crossbody sling bag. It's gone too. And Lily's not here." Annie's eyes darted everywhere—the shadows, the barn doors, the fence line.

"Would she have run off, and Karly had to go look for her?" Daniel held up his hand, stalling Annie's irritated reaction. "I'm only asking. I don't know Lily."

Annie shook her head. "She would never leave Karly's side. Not unless she was in danger or someone took her. She might be four and headstrong, but she follows directions almost to a fault."

Daniel dug his cell phone out of his pocket and dialed the rodeo director, Donovan Keats.

"Hello."

"Daniel Sinclair here. Donovan, I need a favor."

"Name it."

"Gather the rodeo crew at the arena. We have a missing little girl. Those men and women could navigate this place blindfolded."

"On it. Give me ten minutes, and everyone will be there."

"Thanks." Daniel hung up. "We're going to find her."

"We have to. Lily's everything to me." The pain in Annie's voice clawed at his heart.

Izzie gripped his good arm. "Get going on the search for Lily. I'll stay here, but I'm calling Logan to help. When you find that little girl, she'll need the extra comfort only Shadow can give."

"Thanks, sis." Izzie's retired navy SEAL husband would be welcome in the search. And the man's psychiatric service dog Shadow would come in handy. Daniel turned to Annie. "Let's go find your daughter."

The walk through the dusty parking lot to the rodeo arena seemed to drag on forever. Annie had stayed quiet, lost in thought, while Daniel's mind raced with the what-ifs.

As promised, a large group of rodeo participants stood near the arena gate. He recognized most of the regular crew, including Isaac, Ronnie, Courtney, Lena, and rodeo board member Trevor Osborne.

"What's going on, Daniel?" Dayton Carter, a new up-and-coming bull rider, asked.

"First off, let me introduce you to Dr. Anderson Davis. She goes by Annie."

The double takes from the men and the smirks from the women would have been hilarious if the situation weren't so serious. "Her four-year-old daughter is missing. Conor Murray found the babysitter dead a little while ago."

"What can we do to help?"

"Well, let's find her."

"I'm in."

The group all spoke at once.

He held up his hand, stalling further comments. "Thank you for offering to help." That's the response he knew he would get from this group of amazing men and women. "Between the presumed murder, an attack on Annie and me earlier this morning, and the missing girl, I want everyone paired up.

Don't go alone. I don't care if it's daylight or not. We have no idea who we're up against. Check every outbuilding, trailer, and vehicle on the grounds. Don't assume anything. We've had deputies looking for her for a while now with no success. Worst case—someone took Lily. Best case—she's scared and hiding. Don't. I repeat. Don't put yourself in danger. Call for backup if you run into a problem."

The group nodded in agreement.

Annie stepped forward and held her phone out with a picture of Lily on the screen. "She's four. She loves koalas and corn dogs. She hates loud noises and always holds hands when she crosses the street." She inhaled. "Please find her. She's everything to me." Her voice broke on her final words.

Daniel's chest tightened at the raw pain behind her plea. "All right, people, let's get to work. You all have my phone number. If not, see me before you head out. I'll send out Lily's picture. Don't forget to text or call with updates."

The small crowd dispersed on the hunt for the little girl.

He dialed the sheriff's office. "Cory, pull every camera feed from the main gate of the park, along with the fairgrounds and carnival entrance. Get someone to start questioning people around here."

"On it, Deputy. The sheriff called a few minutes ago. She's already put an Amber Alert into play."

He should have known Izzie had taken action when he and Annie left the scene. "Thanks, Cory. Keep me updated."

"Will do, Deputy."

Daniel disconnected the call and turned his attention to Annie. "Are you okay?"

"No." Her honest answer surprised him. "But I will be, once we find Lily."

He guided her toward the exit in silence. Her strength floored him. Beneath the fear, the exhaustion, the injuries, she stood tall. Focused. Resolute.

Outside the arena, Daniel scanned the horizon. His gut twisted into knots. The sun hung low in the sky. Shadows had begun to stretch long and deep between the barns. But they still had several hours of daylight left.

"We're going to find her," he said again, more for his benefit than Annie's. They had to. The other option—unacceptable.

Arms crossed, Annie's fingernails dug into her skin. "If someone hurt my little girl…"

Daniel looked at her. For a moment, the world fell away, and it was just the two of them. "They won't. Not if I have anything to say about it."

"I promised Libby that if anything happened to her and Austin, I'd protect Lily and keep her safe. Raise her right. Now this…" Annie spread her arms, palms up, and spun slowly in a circle. Her eyes combed the area. She fisted her hands. "Where is she? Where's my daughter?"

For the first time since the nightmare had begun, Annie's first tears fell. The strong, determined woman she'd portrayed shattered.

Unable to stop himself, he gathered her in his arms and held her as fear and grief spilled from her eyes.

He couldn't fail his best friend from his youth, and there was no way he could fail another child.

FOUR

Daniel cupped Annie's elbow and escorted her away from the arena into the parking lot. She'd shut down hard after the tears stopped flowing. Fatigue shadowed her features along with worry lines creasing her forehead. But the worst part…she'd gone quiet. Unsure what to do, he walked beside her, giving her a moment to collect herself. As they left the confines of the arena area, he eyed the dried blood on her shirt and pants. He'd swapped his shirt earlier at the sheriff's office with one from his locker, but Annie hadn't had extras with her. If—no, he couldn't think that way—when they found Lily, the last thing the little girl should see was her mom covered in blood.

"Do you have a change of clothes with you?" The daylight faded as they stepped farther into the parking lot.

Annie looked at him like he had three heads. Her dried tears stained her cheeks, compelling him to pull her into another hug, but he resisted. "Um…in my car. I packed everything in my SUV and came straight here this morning. We haven't taken our things to the rental house."

"Why don't we get you cleaned up before we search. We wouldn't want to scare the livestock." He flashed her a cheesy grin. And there he went again. Making a joke. But that's what he did—what people expected of him.

She pulled the hem of her shirt out and studied it. "Guess I do look pretty bad. Why didn't you say something before?"

"Meh, we had other things more important. Car?" He gestured toward the parking lot.

"Over there." She pointed to one of the back spots.

He steered her in the direction she'd indicated. When he spotted the SUV that she'd described, his steps faltered. He expected a moving trailer hitched to her vehicle. "Where's the rest of your stuff?"

"This is it."

"What do you mean? There can't be more than a few boxes and a couple of suitcases in there."

Her chin dipped. "I—I was in a bit of a hurry."

His gaze darted between her and her vehicle. There was a story behind the lack of things, but he didn't have time to pry it out of her. Not with Lily missing. "Grab some clothes. I'll show you to your office where you'll have some privacy. Then we can join the search for Lily."

Annie nodded and collected a gym bag. "Let's hurry. I want to find my daughter."

"Here, let me take that." Daniel took the duffel and slung it over his shoulder.

The pair strode to a small off-white building within stumbling distance to the arena and barn. "That's it over there. It's a modular unit. It has a small reception area attached to a larger exam room with medical supplies, and a bathroom that includes a shower."

Annie remained quiet, no doubt lost in thought about her daughter.

Even with the sun lower in the sky, the heat continued to press down, and dust kicked up with each step they took. His arm throbbed behind the bandage, but he shrugged off the ache. There was no time for pain—not with a little girl missing. Not with his childhood best friend worried about her daughter.

They reached the building labeled Rodeo Medical in bold black letters, and he retrieved the key Keats had given him a little while ago for Annie. He unlocked the door and opened it. The thing creaked on its hinges. A stale odor of antiseptic greeted them. "These are your new digs." He gave her a quick tour. "Go ahead and change. I'll check my messages and see if anyone has news."

She hesitated then disappeared into the bathroom with her bag.

He leaned against the wall instead of sitting on the lone leather couch near the desk and file cabinet and sighed. No new messages. Hope had flared when the rodeo community struck out on their search that they'd find Lily in record time. It hadn't been long, but his optimism took a nosedive.

A few minutes later Annie emerged wearing a clean T-shirt, jean shorts, and her boots. Classic Texas cowgirl.

"These are yours." He handed her the keys to her new office. "Ready."

She accepted them and tucked them into her front pocket and her phone into the back pocket. "Yup."

They exited and Annie locked the door. She pivoted to face him. "Where do we start?"

"How about the fairgrounds and work our way to the carnival?" The distant bleat of goats, the low rumble of an engine, and the cheerful music in the background all betrayed the urgency of finding Lily.

"Lily and Karly planned to go to the petting zoo first."

"Then that's where we start looking."

They entered the barn and made the loop of animals, showing people Lily's picture along the way and asking if they'd seen the girl. A few said yes, but they hadn't seen her in hours.

After exhausting the petting zoo and the livestock barns,

Daniel gestured to the white food tents. "Maybe they got something to eat."

The savory scent of grilled BBQ meat drifting in the air mingled with the sickeningly sweet aroma of cotton candy. The bustle of the people grabbing a meal before enjoying the final few hours of the fair and carnival for the night crowded the area.

He and Annie continued to search and show Lily's picture. Daniel moved behind the tents, closer to the exhibit building and checked every nook and cranny—under every bush and shrub—but came up empty.

"Daniel!" Courtney hollered as she and Lena, two of the young barrel racers, strode toward them.

"Hey ladies, what's up? Did you find anything?"

Courtney's shoulders drooped. "Sorry, no. Lena and I plus a couple of the guys cleared the arena and the loading docks. We even searched under the bleachers. But we didn't find Lily or any clues to where she might be."

"We're heading to the lake next," Lena said.

"Thanks. We appreciate it. But please be careful near the woods. Maybe see if the guys will go with you. You know, safety in numbers." These young women were smart and strong. He had no doubt they could take care of themselves. But he wasn't kidding about the safety in numbers with Karly's death and a knife-wielding masked man on the loose.

"I'll call the guys and keep you posted." Courtney motioned toward the tree-lined path, and she and Lena jogged off.

Annie spun to face him. "Where is she, Daniel?"

With all the hidden corners and tucked away places, Daniel had hoped someone would discover Lily hiding in the arena area. "I wish I could tell you." He hated any crime or emergency related to children. But the intense worry in Annie's tone gripped his heart like a vise.

The crowds buzzed just beyond where they stood. A lone tear trailed down Annie's cheek.

Daniel gently gripped her arms. "Hey, breathe. We'll search every inch of these grounds. She has to be here somewhere."

Annie lifted her head. Fear flickered in her gaze. "I can't lose her. Not after Libby..." A shadow crossed her face. An unpleasant memory, maybe?

"You won't. I promise." And he'd done it again. Promising things he shouldn't. He should stick with humor and stay far away from the serious stuff. It tended to get him into trouble. But the jokes and lighthearted remarks were beyond him right now.

The sun dipped low, hanging on the edge of the horizon. Time was getting away from them, but Daniel hadn't missed her exhaustion. "Let's take a small break then regroup and return to the search."

"I don't want to stop." Annie's voice rose an octave. Her eyes darted around the area.

"I understand that. But you've had a lot going on today, and we've been out here quite a while. We aren't giving up. Just putting a short pause on it. The others are still out there looking for her."

Annie slumped. "You're right. I'm struggling to keep going, but I feel like I'm abandoning her if I stop."

"How about this. We go back to your new office, grab a bottle of water, and take a ten-minute break for you to close your eyes and mentally recharge. It might spark an idea, so we aren't running in circles like a dog chasing his tail."

Her head bobbed up and down. "I could use a moment. But not too long."

"Water and a quick rest. Fifteen minutes, tops. Then we'll head to the carnival." He held out his hand toward her office. "Let's go. I'll call Izzie while we're there."

"Thank you."

"For what?"

"For saving me this morning—twice. For taking Lily's disappearance seriously. For enlisting all those people to look for her. And for being the voice of reason and keeping me from losing my mind."

"I don't know about all that, but we used to be best friends." He clutched her hand. "So, no matter what, I'm here for you."

They walked hand in hand across the parking lot. As they approached her office, she gave him a sad smile. "I'm sorry about how I left—" Her eyes widened. "Daniel!"

He jerked his gaze in the direction of her stare. The door stood open with a view of the inside.

Daniel pushed Annie behind him and withdrew his Sig Sauer. "Stay here." He cleared the small building then focused on the mess. Papers lay strewn across the floor. Cabinet doors yanked open and their contents scattered in a heap. The inside of the desk drawers were in a shambles.

"Annie, come on in, but don't touch anything."

She peeked in and gasped. "Who? Why?"

"I don't know, but I'll call this in and let someone process the scene." He dialed Izzie.

"Sheriff Sinclair."

"Hey, sis. First, any news on Lily?" He didn't think so, but it was worth asking.

"Nothing so far. It's like she vanished."

"Same here." He glanced at Annie and shook his head. "Second, I need a crime scene tech to the rodeo medical office. Someone broke in. It appears whoever picked the lock tossed the place, looking for something in particular. It's a mess, but at first glance, nothing seems to be missing. I'm doing a quick scan, then we'll step out and wait for a deputy to secure the scene. I hate to take manpower away from the search, but if it's linked..." Daniel let the possibility hang.

"I'm sending Deputy McGregor to lock it down. Let him know if you discover what this person was after."

"You got it. Thanks, Izz." Daniel hung up and plucked two sets of exam gloves from the box on the counter. "Here. Once we take a look around, we'll leave McGregor in charge."

Annie donned the gloves. "I have no idea if anything was stolen from the office, so you'll have to determine that. I'll check the bathroom where I left my bag."

He'd seen the open duffel with clothes haphazardly thrown in, but Annie might not be particular about stuff like that. Either way, she could determine if someone riffled through her things. He picked up a single patient file, flipped through it carefully then placed it on the desk. Nothing jumped out at him. He moved to the exam room and scanned the wreckage. The glass doors on the small cabinet that held the pain medication remained locked. Although, who'd be desperate enough to break into that, he had no clue. It only contained basic medicine as of right now. Nothing hardcore.

"Daniel!"

"What's up?" He stepped to the doorway of the bathroom.

Clothes lay on the floor, and Annie sat cross-legged digging through her bag. "Nothing's missing, but the inside of this is a mess. Whoever did this was looking for something."

"Any idea what?"

She stopped rummaging through her duffel and stood. "The only thing in this office that belongs to me are those clothes."

"Then I'm guessing it has to do with the office. Unless…"

Annie shifted to face him. "What?"

"Who knew you were the new rodeo doc?"

"Not many. Donovan Keats, Karly, and whoever processed the paperwork. I only told my mentor, Dr. Gregory, that I got a new job. I didn't say where or what. Even you didn't know it was me."

"That's true." He scratched the stubble on his jaw. "However, you outed yourself at the lake and at the arena. Plus, whoever did this could have seen us come in here."

"So, this is about me?" Her brows pulled together. "Wait. What about the key? Could someone have seen Deputy Bonner give it to me?"

Daniel itched his upper lip with the back of his wrist. "This all circles back to the attack at the lake."

"It's the only thing that makes sense. Why else would someone break into this office now?" Annie's wide eyes stared at him.

She had a point. But… "If that's the case, how does it connect to Lily? Or does it?"

If the man responsible for attacking Annie had her daughter, then the urgency to find the girl had ramped up to a white-knuckled bull ride level.

Annie shook from the adrenaline coursing through her. Deputy McGregor had taken over the crime scene twenty minutes ago, and she and Daniel moved to the carnival to continue the search for Lily. The high-pitched whimsical music filled the air, a cheerful contradiction to the dread stirring in her belly. The absence of her daughter's giggles and Lily's tiny hand tucked into hers clawed grooves in her heart.

Daniel laced his fingers with hers as they wove through the horde of people. "Is it always this busy?" Annie's attention jerked from one sound to the next.

"The rodeo board promoted the events like crazy. I'm guessing that's the reason for the larger crowds this year." He glanced at their hands. "You're trembling."

"I'm sorry."

"No reason to be sorry." He studied her a moment then let the comment drop.

Tension coiled in her belly. Families laughed and played. The entire scene felt…off. Clowns tied balloon animals and juggled bowling pins, entertaining the children and adults alike. A blur of color caught her attention. She spun to investigate. Nothing.

"Annie, what's wrong?" Daniel flipped his gaze to her.

"Just a weird sensation." Ignoring the paranoia that had set in, Annie refocused on the search for Lily.

"We'll head around back once we walk through the main carnival area. Keep your eyes out for anywhere a child could hide or be hidden."

She nodded.

People pressed around them. A child dropped a cheap teddy bear he must have won at a game booth.

Daniel retrieved the stuff animal and knelt in front of the boy. "Here ya go."

"Thank you." The child eyed Daniel's badge, striking up a conversation between man and boy.

Annie smiled at the interaction. A hand brushed her arm, jerking her attention away from the tender scene. A clown with a horrible makeup job cracked a smile then latched on to her wrist and yanked her off balance. Before she could pull in a lung full of air to scream, he dragged her away from the crowd and between two games.

"Help!" The blaring music and the joyous screams of carnival goers drowned out her plea.

Gloved hands wrapped her neck and squeezed. "What did that cop tell you? He gave you something, didn't he?"

Her lungs struggled to pull in air. Panic surged through her chest. Strangled rasps wheezed past his grip on her throat. She raked her fingernails at his fabric-covered arms.

Think, Annie. Don't freeze.

"Annie!" Daniel's voice broke through her terror. He was close. She just had to survive until he found her.

Her vision tunneled. Spots danced at the edges.

She wrenched sideways, twisting. Anything to loosen the

clown's grip. Her hand patted the ground, desperate to find a weapon of any kind to use. Her fingers closed on something—a broken piece of wood. Splinters from the rough surface slid into her palm. With the little strength she had remaining, she swung it at her attacker.

The sharp edge connected with his temple.

He howled and loosened his grip enough for air to rush back into her lungs.

She sucked in oxygen. "Daniel!"

The reprieve didn't last long. The clown's hands found her throat again and tightened. Fury blazed in his eyes. "That's it. I don't care what you know or who you told. You're dead."

"Annie!" The thunder of Daniel's voice gave her hope.

The man spun too late. Daniel yanked him off her, and the guy's grip vanished. She crumpled to the ground and clutched her throat.

Daniel grappled with the attacker. The clown twisted free, slammed a shoulder into Daniel, and bolted toward the maze of rides. Chest heaving, Daniel rushed to her side. He dropped to his knees.

"I'm okay," she croaked.

"You're not. This is the third time someone has tried to kill you." His voice was a rough mix of rage and fear. "He almost—" His teeth clenched.

Annie swallowed against the burn in her throat. Her pulse still thundered in her ears. "He thinks I know something. He wanted me dead."

Daniel's gaze flicked to the shadows where the man had vanished, then back to her. "Not on my watch."

He helped her to her feet and scanned the crowd. He pulled out his phone. "I'm requesting medical."

"No. I'll be okay. Lily is more important than a few bruises."

"Annie."

"Please, don't." She didn't have the energy to argue.

The war within was written on Daniel's face. "All right. Stay close. Tell me if you change your mind about the paramedics."

"I promise." And she would. As a doctor she knew what signs to look for. If she were dead, she couldn't help her daughter.

"I don't like it. But I understand and won't push. However, I *am* calling Izzie. She needs to know." He contacted his sister and reported what happened. When he finished, he slipped his hand into hers. "Then let's find your daughter." He led her to the alley behind the carnival. His attention appeared to be split between looking for Lily and the man who'd attacked her.

A few moments after searching under and around several games, Daniel exhaled. "Are you doing okay?"

"The skin where he grabbed me is hot. I can tell it's bruised even without looking." She touched her neck. Her pulse raced. What if the guy in the clown costume came back to finish her off?

"Tell me about Lily." Daniel's request took her off guard.

She shook the lingering fear aside—for the moment—and checked under the backside of another game. Thick electrical wires crisscrossed along the grassy ground where the trailers had dug deep ruts. Annie hadn't expected to find Lily there, but her heart dropped all the same. "Well, she's four and the sweetest little girl you've ever met. She's super smart. Of course, I might be a bit biased." Annie smiled at him. "Lily is a chatterbox. Inquisitive. And makes friends wherever she goes."

Daniel checked another section of maintenance row, but she hadn't missed how he continued to scan the surroundings. "She sounds amazing."

"She is. I can't imagine life without her." Annie's voice cracked.

"I—"

"Daniel! Annie, are you okay?" Izzie and a man with a black Labrador who Annie had never met strode toward them.

"I'm sore, but alive. I'm more worried about Lily at the moment than a few bruises." Annie wouldn't admit that the fear from the attempt on her life threatened to erupt.

"I called Rollins PD and requested additional officers to come scour the carnival."

"Thanks, sis. I'm not a fan of Annie being out in the open, but with Lily missing…" Daniel shrugged. "Annie, this is Izzie's husband, retired navy SEAL Logan Russell, and his service dog, Shadow."

"Nice to meet you. Izzie told me what happened today and about your daughter. I'm sorry I couldn't get here sooner, but Shadow and I were out of town for work." Logan patted the dog's head.

Annie managed a grateful smile as Shadow padded forward. He nudged her. She ran a hand over his fur. The dog's presence was grounding—a silent force of calm in the chaos.

"Shadow's a PTSD service dog, not a tracker, but he has great instincts," Logan said.

"Thank you for coming." Annie appreciated all the help she could get.

"If we work together, we can cover more ground." Izzie waved to the backlot of the carnival. "I brought stronger flashlights since the sun is almost down."

"Thanks." Daniel accepted the additional lights, handed one to Annie, and used his to gesture to where they'd already checked for hiding places. "We've cleared that area over there."

"Since the rest of the rodeo community and my deputies have the fairgrounds covered and the main carnival area, let's stick to here." Izzie pointed to the space between the trailers and trucks. "You two take that side, we'll take this one."

"Let's do this." Logan placed his hand on the small of Izzie's back, and the pair plus Shadow got started.

She and Daniel moved to the next section. Their beams illuminated the darkened corners of the service corridor.

The night pressed down, squeezing the air from Annie's lungs. Her poor daughter. Out there alone. Scared.

Please don't let her be hurt.

The group continued behind the community building that held the 4-H exhibits and the horticulture contests. A faded city park shed came into view, tucked between two overgrown shrubs. Weathered wood with rusted hinges greeted them. An old padlock dangled from the door, loose and cockeyed.

Izzie strode over, her flashlight beam sweeping the ground. "Anything?"

"No. You?" Daniel asked.

"Not a single clue." Izzie sighed.

Annie wanted to scream. "I get that I might be in this guy's crosshairs after this morning, but I don't understand why he would take Lily? How would he know I have a daughter?"

"That's a great question. I'm not sure he did. If she witnessed what happened to Karly, she could have run away."

"I know you're trying to make me feel better by saying she's lost somewhere, but face it, whoever killed Karly probably took Lily."

Shadow growled.

"What's up with him?" Daniel pointed to the Lab.

The dog stiffened, then bolted toward the shed.

"Shadow, wait—" Logan called, but the dog stopped short of the old building and pawed at the wooden door.

Annie's breath caught. "Lily?" Her voice cracked. She tried again. "Lily!"

No answer.

Daniel stepped forward, slipped off the open padlock, and jiggled the handle. "It's stuck."

"I got it." Logan knelt in front of the door and withdrew a

wicked-looking utility knife from his cargo pants. He worked the latch until it gave way. The door creaked open.

Daniel swept his light around the interior and froze. "Annie."

She joined him at the entrance. "Lily!" Curled in the corner, her daughter blinked up and flinched at the light. Annie dropped to her knees. Heart in her throat, she gave her daughter a quick once-over. Dirt streaked her face, but other than that, Lily didn't appear to have any noticeable injuries. She gathered the little girl into her arms. "Baby, it's me. Mommy's here."

Lily wrapped her tiny arms around Annie's neck and clung tight. Her little body trembled. When Annie drew back to look at her daughter's precious face, Lily's lower lip quivered.

"I'm so glad we found you." Annie squeezed her one more time. "What happened?"

Lily tucked her head into the crook of Annie's neck.

"Honey?"

Lily's arms tightened, and she held on like a baby monkey.

Daniel crouched beside them. "Hey, sweetheart. We've been looking everywhere for you."

The little girl rolled her head and peeked at Daniel but stayed quiet.

Shadow nosed forward, nudging Lily's hand. After a long pause, her tiny fingers curled into his fur. One shaky stroke. Then another.

"Any signs of injury?" Izzie asked from outside the shed.

Annie shook her head. "Just fear. I didn't see any wounds, but I'll take a closer look once we get her out of here."

"I'll call the paramedics." Logan removed his cell phone from his pocket.

Tightening her hold, Annie glanced up at Logan. "No. I'm a doctor. She's staying with me." No one would take her baby away from her. If Lily required medical attention, she'd either provide it, or accompany her to the hospital. The trauma would be another story. But physical injuries, Annie could handle.

Daniel placed a hand on Annie's shoulder. "It's okay. No one is taking her from you."

"Thank you." Annie shivered. The shed seemed colder now. And in the heat of August that didn't make sense. She chalked it up to the fade of adrenaline.

Shadow whined and nudged Lily.

The girl leaned over, latched on to Shadow's neck, and refused to let go.

Daniel's warm hand rested on Annie's back. "What do you say we get Lily back to Stone Creek Ranch and feed her."

"I think that's a great idea." With Daniel's help, Annie peeled Lily away from the dog and stood with her daughter in her arms. Shadow plastered himself to her leg and watched Lily like a sentinel.

"It appears we'll be joining you." Logan jutted his chin toward his dog.

"Appreciate that." Daniel nodded.

"Go on. Get them back to the ranch. I'll take care of things here."

"Thanks, Izzie." Daniel escorted Annie and her daughter away from the nightmare of the shed to the parking lot.

Annie's emotions had taken a ride on the carnival's scrambler and refused to get off. Her nerves had hit the limit, and she hung on to her sanity by a thread. Annie had escaped one mess to fall into the depths of another.

FIVE

Lily's arms wrapped around Annie's neck. The tightness of her hold pressed against the bruises from the earlier attack. Her throat ached, but she wouldn't tell Lily to let go. The day had lasted too long and had pushed both her and her daughter to their limits. They both needed somewhere to decompress, and from what she remembered of Stone Creek Ranch, it was just the place to do that. However, she required their suitcases.

Too tired to move items, she sighed. "Daniel, I need to take my car. All of our belongings are in it, along with Lily's booster seat."

"We could move everything to my truck."

"Daniel." *Please, don't make me do one more thing.*

"I hate you driving all the way to the ranch after what happened."

Yeah, well, join the club, but she had no intention of transferring all her stuff to his truck. Besides, she didn't want to leave her SUV here overnight.

He rubbed the back of his neck. "I suppose it makes sense though. Do you remember how to get there?"

"Sort of. It's been a long time." She had a general idea but hadn't visited the ranch in years.

"I'd rather trail you but since you aren't sure of the way, follow me." He held out his hand. "Keys, please. I'll unlock your car, so you don't have to juggle Lily and open the doors."

She handed him the keys she'd tucked into her pocket hours ago. "That would be helpful."

The back door open, Annie pried Lily's arms off her. "It's okay, sweetie. We're going to a friend's house."

Lily's blank stare concerned her. The girl complied, and Annie pulled the strap across her and buckled it.

"Give me a second then follow closely. I want you in my sight at all times."

"I will." Annie started her car. "Lily, we're going to a really cool ranch house. I'll give you a bath, then maybe you can tell me what happened." Annie glanced in the rearview mirror, hoping for a response. None came.

They rolled away from the park and headed down the country highway not long after. The darkness surrounded her, setting her on edge. Daniel's taillights shone like two red eyes glowing in the dark fifty yards ahead. When his truck rose over a small hill and the lights disappeared, it was the longest few seconds of her life before they came into view again.

"Lily, you're going to love Miss Hannah. That's Mr. Daniel's mom. She's really nice." Annie flicked her gaze to her daughter.

Headlights popped over the same small hill behind her. Annie's pulse spiked. Her fingers dug into the steering wheel in a white-knuckle grip. How long had that vehicle been back there? Had her laser focus on Daniel's truck and her silent daughter caused her to miss someone following them?

Heart pounding, her eyes shifted from the road ahead to the one behind. She leaned forward for a better look in the mirror. The lights grew. The vehicle closed in—fast.

"Please, go around. Please," Annie begged.

A truck rammed her bumper. The sudden jolt rocked her SUV.

"Hold on, Lily!"

The next hit struck the driver's side back corner. Her SUV

veered to the right, knocking her onto the shoulder of the road. The tires skidded in the loose gravel, sending the vehicle into the ditch. Tall brush and tree limbs scraped the exterior. Doing her best to slow down, she bounced over ruts and struck the low embankment, flinging herself forward. Her seat belt snapped tight across her body, sending her back into her seat. Pain radiated through her torso.

Lily whimpered but never cried out.

"Hold on, baby." Annie blinked, willing the haze to clear.

The back door popped open with a groan.

She had help. Daniel had seen her run off the road. He'd take care of everything. She twisted in time to see a tall man yank Lily from her seat. Not Daniel. Her pulse spiked.

"No! Leave her alone!" The nighttime obscured the view of his face.

"Get out if you want your daughter to live."

Her heart hammered against her sore ribs. "I'm coming. Please don't hurt her." She struggled with the handle. Maybe if she stalled it would give Daniel time to rescue them.

"Hurry up."

"I'm sorry, but I'm shaking." She hadn't lied. Her hands resembled a leaf in a windstorm. The entire situation scared her to death. She released the latch and tumbled from the SUV. Her body protested the movement.

A car engine roared, coming in her direction, and tires skidded on the road.

The man took off into the trees with her daughter.

She scrambled around the car to go after him.

"Annie!"

Gasping for air, she pointed to where the man had run off. "He's gone. He has Lily!"

Daniel sprinted to his truck and grabbed a flashlight. She noticed his duty weapon in his other hand as well. "Lock yourself in my truck and call Izzie!" He took off into the woods where the man had disappeared with her daughter.

Annie hurried to her SUV. The cup holder where her phone usually rested was empty. She patted around on the floorboard until her hand touched the cool metal. She retrieved her phone then crawled into his truck and locked the doors.

Fingers trembling, she dialed Izzie's number.

"Sheriff Sinclair."

"Izzie, It's me. Annie. He has Lily."

"Slow down. Who has Lily, and where is Daniel?"

"Someone ran me off the road and took my daughter. Daniel went after him. He told me to lock myself in his truck and call you."

"We're on our way. Don't leave that truck." The line went dead.

Annie desperately wanted to search for Lily. It took everything in her to stay in place and not go running into the woods to help find her daughter.

Staring into the darkness, she prayed Daniel would save her daughter before it was too late.

Daniel's heart raced as he plunged into the trees. His flashlight cut swaths through the dark. The brush crunched under his boots, joining his ragged breath. Why hadn't he insisted that Annie and Lily ride with him and asked Logan to drive her SUV to the ranch? He wanted to yell at the stupid decision that could cost Lily her life. Regret seeped in and grabbed hold.

God, please, let me get to her in time.

Keeping the beam low on the ground, he swung the flashlight side to side in his frantic search for the man who'd taken Lily. A thousand needles accompanied the heat that surged over his chest. Panic threatened to overtake him. *Slow down and think. Act like a deputy and not an untrained civilian.* Charging blind was a rookie mistake. One he couldn't afford to make. He crouched, tuned into the sounds, and scanned the darkness for movement. A twig popped behind him. He swung around, but his light flashed across nothing but tree trunks. He pivoted again. It was too quiet—too still.

Daniel continued to listen. Branches snapped. The muffled thud of footsteps swung his attention to his left. But it was a child's faint whimper that tore him in two.

Target narrowed in, he hurried toward the pair, dodging low-hanging branches that threatened to claw his face. Movement caught his eye. A shadow flitting between the old oaks. He shifted left, tried to cut him off, but the man doubled back, darting deeper into the woods.

The game of cat and mouse that could end with deadly results if he didn't stop the man made his stomach churn. He refused to let another child down.

The crunch of gravel popped through the night. An engine roared to life. Daniel sprinted toward the sound. Branches scraped his arms and tore at the bandage, but he didn't care. He burst through the tree line in time to see taillights bouncing down the road.

"No!" He'd allowed the man to take Lily. He prayed Annie had called Izzie as he'd requested.

"Daniel!" Annie ran toward him. "Did you find Lily?"

He pointed at the cloud of dust settling.

Annie shook her head. "He didn't have her when he got in his truck. He—he didn't take Lily."

"Are you certain?"

"She wasn't with him." Annie's voice cracked. "She's still here. Somewhere."

Red-and-blue lights bounced off the trees. A sheriff's SUV sped down the road in the opposite direction from the suspect. Tires squealed and doors slammed.

"Daniel!" Izzie. She'd arrived a minute too late to catch

the guy, but they had a little girl to find and could use all the help they could get.

"Over here." He and Annie waited by his truck. The interior light glowed, allowing them to see each other.

Izzie and Logan strode to them. "Report."

"Our mystery man caused Annie to run off the road. He grabbed Lily and took off into the woods."

"He wanted me to go with him, but Daniel scared him off." She rubbed her hands up and down her arms as if chilled. But the temperature couldn't be lower than seventy-five or eighty degrees.

Logan gaze swept the tree line. "You think Lily's still out there?"

Annie nodded. "When the guy left the woods, he didn't have her in his arms."

"Then let's split up and find her." Izzie's take-charge sheriff persona surfaced.

"Annie, stay with me." Daniel cupped her elbow and guided her to the trees. "Call out if you find her."

"Will do." Logan waved and vanished into the woods.

"That man does stealth like nobody's business. First, he's there. Then he's gone. It's kinda scary." Izzie blew out a breath and, not as quietly, strode deeper into the woods.

"Let's find Lily." Daniel gestured to the dark interior of the trees.

They walked side by side using the flashlights to search in the brush.

"Lily!" Annie's desperate cry broke his heart. A while later, she stopped. "Why can't we find her? You don't think he…?"

"No. I don't." He hated that Annie's mind had gone to the worst-case scenario. Daniel's throat tightened. He swept his light at a tight grouping of trees and froze. A small figure huddled against one of the trunks. Arms wrapped around her knees, Lily's wide eyes stared back at him.

"Found her." Daniel jutted his chin at the little girl.

Annie rushed over and scooped Lily into her arms. Unable to balance, Annie plopped onto the ground.

Daniel joined them and knelt in the dirt. "Hey, kiddo. You're safe now."

She didn't speak. Didn't blink. Just clung tighter to Annie.

He twisted and yelled over his shoulder. "Izzie! Logan! We found her!"

The pair appeared a few moments later.

"I'll call the paramedics." Izzie lifted her cell phone and placed the request.

For the first time since Annie returned to Rollins, she didn't protest the medical help.

Assisting Annie to stand, he escorted her to his truck while they waited on the medic unit to arrive. He popped the tailgate down and padded it with a blanket. The paramedics would need room to work. "Have a seat. I'll find another blanket. Although it might smell like horse." He lifted the mother-daughter duo onto the tailgate.

A slight smile curved Annie's lips. "Thanks."

Several minutes later, the paramedics hustled over.

"So, this is the cutie we've heard about." Harper unzipped her duffel. "May I take a look?"

Annie nodded but Lily didn't let go. "Baby, this nice lady would like to see your ouchies. It's okay. She'll be gentle." She lifted her gaze and raised a brow at Harper.

"Of course. I'm better at owies than this lug." Harper jerked her head toward Noah.

"Hey, now. Don't let her fool you, Lily. I'm the best."

The little girl's eyes darted from one medic to the other. She didn't smile or talk but released Annie's neck.

Daniel hung back as Harper and Noah did their thing. He sent up a prayer of thanks that they'd found Lily and that Noah examined Annie's prior injuries as well as the current ones.

Exhaustion etched every line of Annie's face, but she didn't let go of Lily. Not for a second.

As Daniel stood there, he promised himself one thing—he would find whoever came after that little girl and her mother and see to it the man was thrown in jail.

Steam snaked upward from the cup of coffee Daniel held below his chin. He sat at his mother's kitchen table and let the bold aroma permeate his senses. Between the scent of the brew and the infusion of caffeine, he prayed his brain engaged sooner versus later. He'd woken up to Lily's screams in the middle of the night. It took everything in him to resist the urge to run and help Annie calm her daughter. But Lily had her mom and Shadow. She didn't need him. He, on the other hand, had no one to calm the terror running through him at the *what could have happened* thoughts invading his mind. So, instead, he'd laid in bed, staring at the ceiling. Regret had washed over him, and when he'd fallen asleep, the nightmares of another child's screams plagued him. Normally, he'd help his mom with ranch chores to work off the tension, but she'd waved him off, telling him to take care of his friend and her adorable little girl. For once in his life, he had no desire to spend time outside with the animals.

"Morning." Annie carried Lily in and sat across the table. Shadow trailed the pair and plopped onto the floor next to them.

"Good morning. I won't ask if you slept well." His eyes locked on to her daughter. The girl's hair reminded him of the rat's nest in the old shed out in the back forty.

Annie gave him a knowing smile. "What are the plans for the day?"

"Izzie's coming over to discuss your case. Or maybe I should say both of your cases." He waggled a finger between the two of them. "I better take Shadow out and let him do his business. He may look relaxed, but the lump of fur is probably crossing his doggy legs."

"I'm sorry, boy. I'm not used to animals." Annie scratched the dog's head.

"Come on, Shadow." Daniel made his way to the door. "When I get back, I'll feed you."

"Who are you referring to?" Annie smirked.

What was the woman talking about? Then it hit him, and he glanced at Shadow and laughed. "All of you, I suppose." Shaking his head, he opened the back door and let the dog out into the yard. A few minutes later when they returned, he noticed Annie and Lily hadn't moved. "Are you still awake?"

"Barely." Annie laid her cheek on Lily's head.

He fed Shadow and retrieved the plate of pastries from the counter and the pan of bacon from the oven where he'd kept the meat warm. "It's not mom's normal spread, but it's comfort food."

"I'm all about that today."

"Has she…?" Daniel didn't want to ask in front of Lily, but he was dying to know if the girl had spoken yet.

Annie shook her head.

Growing up during those awkward teenage years, they'd always been able to read each other's thoughts. Apparently, at least for the moment, that hadn't changed. A little while later, he gestured to Shadow, who'd trotted to the back door. "I'm taking him outside."

Annie tilted her head. "Didn't he just go?"

"Logan usually lets him run for a few minutes after breakfast before he starts work. Guess Shadow doesn't want to miss out on chasing a couple of rabbits. Be right back."

"I don't plan on going anywhere." Annie rested her chin on Lily's head and closed her eyes.

"Fair enough." Daniel let Shadow outside and followed the furball. The screen door creaked closed behind him. He stood on the back porch of the ranch house while the dog sniffed around the bushes and ran circles in the yard. The scent of hay and animals clung to the morning breeze. He breathed in the mind-clearing aroma, but the silence sat heavy on his shoulders. Too quiet, even for his family's ranch. He rubbed the back of his neck, watching the sunlight stretch across the dewy fields. Peace should've inhabited the stillness, but this morning it felt more like the world held its breath in anticipation of the proverbial other shoe to drop.

When he returned inside with Shadow in tow, he and Annie moved to the living room. Daniel piled blankets on the floor for Lily.

Annie lay her daughter on the makeshift bed. Shadow nestled beside her like a living weighted blanket. Daniel motioned to the couch. Annie lowered herself onto the cushion and positioned herself in full view of Lily. She hadn't moved far from her daughter since they'd brought the young girl home. Daniel got it. He really did. Yesterday's events had been traumatic for both of them. He wished for a way to eliminate the fear for the pair.

"Hello!" Izzie poked her head into the living room. "Did you save me any coffee?"

"Like Mom doesn't have a backup bag of grounds to her backup bag." He rolled his eyes. Their mom had learned early on to have more than enough coffee if she wanted chores done in a timely manner. "Oh, hey, Logan." Izzie's husband stood in the doorway to the room.

Index and middle finger touching his brow, Logan gave him a two-finger salute then headed straight for the kitchen and the coffeepot. Izzie chuckled and disappeared around the corner.

The couple returned and sat on the love seat across from him and Annie.

Daniel eyed his brother-in-law. "He's talkative today."

"A morning person he is not." Izzie gave her husband a cheesy smile. "Plus, civilian life is making him soft."

The man lifted his coffee and glared at his wife over the rim of his mug.

Izzie laughed.

Annie's eyes traveled from Logan to Daniel's sister.

"Don't let her fool you, Annie. Logan's a retired navy SEAL. The man 'does' mornings." Daniel's brow furrowed, and he flipped his gaze to Logan. "So, why *do* you look like death warmed over?"

"Your sister drank too much caffeine and wouldn't stop talking to me, so my research took twice as long." Logan's eyes connected with Daniel's then flicked to Shadow and back to him as the man sipped his dark brew.

Ah, the SEAL didn't want to admit in front of Annie that he'd had nightmares or flashbacks and didn't have Shadow's help. Daniel nodded his understanding. Logan's statement about Izzie's nighttime motormouth escapades might be true, but he'd left out the real reason for the zombie impersonation. "We all know what the caffeine boost does to Izzie late at night. I feel for you, man."

"Hey!" Izzie tossed a throw pillow at him. "No ganging up on me."

Lily hadn't moved from where she lay on the floor with Shadow, but Daniel noticed the little one had woken up, her curious gaze tracking his, Izzie, and Logan's conversation. A few moments later her eyes drooped shut again. Yesterday had traumatized the child. At least the poor thing was able to sleep. Of course, Shadow next to her side helped.

Logan tipped his mug toward Lily. "How's…?" He left the question hanging.

"She still hasn't said a word." Annie's eyes drifted to the sleeping Lily.

"Nothing?" Izzie asked.

Annie shook her head. "Shadow has attached himself to her. That's seemed to help. But speaking is beyond her abilities right now for some reason. Normally she's a chatterbox."

The group grew quiet again.

He leaned in. "You okay?"

Annie met his gaze. "Define *okay*."

"Enough said." He wouldn't push. No need. Annie was far from good.

They both looked toward the small girl curled up on the blanket, her fingers clutching Shadow's fur like a lifeline. Her eyes fluttered but didn't open.

"I hate that someone did this to her," he whispered.

"I hate that she's too scared to speak. Too scared to be by herself. I thought…" Annie's voice broke.

"You're not alone in this, Annie. Neither of you are." Izzie pinned her gaze on Daniel.

He blinked at his sister. His normal joke died on his lips. What did she know? And how did she know it? He hadn't told anyone about his nightmares or the reasons for them. Those were his secrets. He didn't need or want his family's pity.

Izzie tucked her leg under her. "We have to figure this out before someone else gets hurt."

Logan clasped Izzie's hand. "I checked in with the hired ranch hands when we arrived. They promised that no one will get on the ranch without their knowledge."

"Thanks." Daniel appreciated his brother-in-law's attentiveness. "I talked with Garrett last night after we arrived." He glanced at Annie. "He's our ranch foreman. Anyway, with everything that happened over the last year, he's on high alert." Daniel's FBI brother, Cooper, had had critter cams put up around the ranch when he and his wife, Grace, dodged a crazed killer almost a year ago. Then Izzie had become the target of a serial killer while she and Logan investigated his twin sister's disappearance. Both cases had positive endings, but for a while everyone had their doubts.

"I'll admit, I'm a bit paranoid after almost losing Izzie and my sister Lisa. I plan to add security measures around our farm at some point in the near future." Logan glanced at Shadow then at Izzie. The man's PTSD apparently still had a strong hold on him.

Izzie nodded her agreement. "As much as I don't like the reasoning, it would help us both sleep better at night." She gave her husband a knowing look, then turned her attention to Daniel and Annie. "I have your statements about the attack at the lake and the one at the carnival, plus the attempted abduction. As for the attacker at the lake and carnival, there's no evidence that he's an immediate danger, only to Deputy Bonner and you. Well, now, just you since Bonner didn't make it. But my deputies are taking turns showing a presence at the park along with the hired security just in case he decides to threaten someone else."

"Keats hired more security guards. This time from GracePoint," Logan added. "They're good at what they do. Grace only hires the best."

Annie's brow scrunched. "Grace. As in Cooper's Grace? She has a security business?"

Daniel nodded. "She's the owner of GracePoint Security. The company offers private investigation and security services. Even law enforcement agencies hire her to help with research and analysis. Logan works for her as well."

"You do?" Annie stared at the retired navy SEAL.

"After an incident overseas and injuries…" Logan paused and zoned out for a moment. When Izzie gently squeezed his knee, he shook his head and continued. "I didn't re-up due to medical reasons and came home to Rollins. Izzie and I worked together to save my twin sister from a serial killer, and the rest they say is history." He lifted Izzie's hand and kissed the back of it.

"Yeah, and they've been mushy ever since." Daniel pretended to stick his finger down his throat and made gagging sounds.

Annie elbowed him gently in the ribs. "Stop it. I think it's great."

"Ow. I'm injured, remember?" He rubbed his side, laying it on thick.

Her eyebrow rose. "That was your other side. Doctor, remember?"

"Watch out, bro. She has your number." Izzie grinned.

"That she does. Always had when she lived here." He couldn't help the smile that bloomed on his lips. His world might never set straight after his life experiences, but Annie had come back to Rollins, and it had started rotating again. She returned his smile, making his heart flutter.

Izzie cleared her throat. "Let's talk through the events. Since we have information about the original attack at the lake, let's start with the break-in at the rodeo medical building. Who knew you're the new doctor, Annie?"

"Donovan Keats, of course, and whoever completed the paperwork for my job, along with Karly. But that's all I know of. My friend and mentor, Dr. Gregory, knew I'd found another job up north..." Annie nibbled on her lower lip "...after my colleague Dr. Pope made threats against Lily and me, but I didn't tell him where or what. Nor did I tell anyone else I used to work with. Although Karly was Gregory's niece, so she might have said something. However, she promised she hadn't told her uncle."

Daniel's jaw dropped. Had he heard her correctly? "Wait. What threats? Who's Dr. Pope."

"Oh, um." She closed her eyes and grimaced like she regretted her words.

"Is that the reason you moved here? A threat from this Pope guy?" His voice rose. She moved here to escape danger? His stomach threatened to revolt.

Izzie pinned him with a glare. "Daniel."

Yeah, okay, so he'd reacted without thinking. "Sorry. What happened to drive you away from your previous job?" There, he'd asked calmly. Yeah, he'd go with that.

Annie looked up through her lashes and remained quiet. Her gaze shifted to her sleeping daughter and back to him. Hesitation evident in her eyes.

Daniel laced his fingers with hers and squeezed. He was playing with fire without a suppression system. She had a kid, and he'd decided a few years back he never—ever—wanted children. Regret still hung heavy over his head and probably always would. He refused to allow himself to get attached to Annie and her daughter. Even if it killed him.

So why was he holding her hand?

Annie's heart raced at the thought of telling her story. For all intents and purposes, she was a private person. Her mother had drummed it into her. No, that wasn't right. She'd shamed her into silence, twisting Annie's pain into selfishness. Crying made you weak. Voicing an opinion made you ungrateful. And if you so much as stepped out of line in front of one of her new boyfriends, the fallout came swift and brutal. A look. A hissed threat. The silent treatment would stretch for days. Few people knew about her family life. Annie had hidden it well. She tended to swallow the words, paste on a smile, and pretend the cracks didn't exist. Once she left for college, her dysfunctional family state developed a neon sign. But she loved her mom…well, because, hello, it was her mother. Then she met Ethan. Annie thought she'd found her forever with him, until he walked away because of Lily.

"It's okay, Annie. You're safe with us. Tell us what happened." Daniel's words jerked her from her thoughts.

Had he zeroed in on her past? Daniel had a knack for sensing when something bothered her. She tucked her doubts and fears away. "A few months ago, I noticed Dr. Layton Pope acting strange. At first, I really didn't think anything of it. I chalked it up to fatigue. A normal occurrence in the emergency department. Overworked, understaffed, and dealing with lives unraveling before our eyes. But over the next few weeks, his actions continued to nag at me."

"Anything specific?" Izzie asked.

Annie pursed her lips. "Little mistakes like forgetting to chart dosages for the nurses then snapping at them for asking. Vanishing for long stretches during his shifts. One time I spotted him meeting a car out by the loading dock."

"Then what?" Daniel encouraged her.

"Soon after, I noticed his hands shaking during an emergency, due to a multicar accident, that lasted over eight hours. We barely had time to go to the bathroom and grab drinks and snacks to keep us going. That's the event that heightened my concerns."

Logan's eyes closed. "Withdrawal."

"Yes. But I didn't have proof. So, from then on, I documented everything until I had enough evidence to present to my mentor, Dr. Todd Gregory. He reviewed my notes, requested the security video of the loading dock, and alerted the director of the hospital board along with local law enforcement. Pope was arrested about a week ago for possession and being under the influence of fentanyl while practicing medicine."

Annie took in a deep breath and continued. "He threatened to hurt Lily and me for reporting him to the police and ruining his career. Dr. Gregory supported me in finding another job away from San Antonio and helped me find childcare to get out of Layton's line of fire, so to speak, until he was safely behind bars for a long time. I told my mentor I found a job up north. He recommended his niece—Karly—since she lived in Dallas and was home from college for the summer and could travel anywhere. I counted on it being safe since my mom never claimed to live in Rollins for whatever reason. No one knew that I ever lived here. It's like she erased those years from our lives."

Hurt flashed across Daniel's face. "No one in San Antonio knows that you lived here?"

"Not that I'm aware of. As far as everyone's concerned, I'm from Houston."

"You said Dr. Pope threatened you. How?" Izzie shifted on the love seat and snuggled into the corner.

"He didn't specify. Just said that he'd hurt Lily and me for turning him in. I'd say he made idle threats, but the hate in his eyes…" Annie shivered at the memory. "If his look was any indication, the man had murderous intentions."

The room quieted. Only the dog's snores filled the space.

Several moments later, Logan spoke. "So, this Pope guy wouldn't know where to find you?"

"I wouldn't put it past him. He's resourceful. But my initial reaction is no. I don't see how. He got out on bail yesterday. Probably too occupied inventing a way to get out of the charges."

"You need to stay vigilant and not ignore this man's threats. I'll do a little discreet investigating into his whereabouts and updates on his case. Dr. Pope has the motive to come after you. He's definitely a suspect in Karly's murder with his link to Lily and fentanyl, but I highly doubt he's the one that actually killed her or that he's our masked man who stabbed Bonner. Pope would be focused on you and Lily, not the others." Izzie tapped on her phone, taking notes. "We can't rule out that Bonner and Karly's deaths are connected. Let's move to the attacks. Both separately and together, and think of other potential suspects."

Logan leaned forward. "Donovan Keats, since he knew about Annie's situation, but I can't for the life of me think of a motive. The carnival manager and any carnies. If one of them found out, they might have tipped off someone else about Bonner's undercover gig. And since the rodeo and carnival travel together a lot, throw in any vendors or contract workers. It could be a coincidence Karly was killed around the same time that Annie showed up. Or it could be related."

"Who found Karly's body again?" Annie's brain had turned to mush. She had a hard time remembering the past twenty-four hours with everything that happened.

"Conor Murray, the owner of Canyon Ridge Gear, a tack and gear vendor in this region." Daniel scratched his jaw. The man looked exhausted. Annie wondered if he'd slept at all last night. "He found her behind the old barn and called it in. I don't think he ever said why he was back there."

Izzie exchanged a glance with Logan. "According to Deputy Bennett, the man was oddly calm. I'd like to reinterview him now that we have more information about Karly's death."

"Speaking of Karly. I'm making an assumption here, but I get the feeling that she hid Lily." Annie had no other logical explanation for Lily being in that shed. "How did she know to do that?"

"That's a great question. And I tend to agree with that theory. The killer wouldn't have left a witness alive." Izzie studied the floor like it would produce an answer.

"I can only think of two possibilities. One, someone came after them, but I have no clue why. Two, they witnessed something, and Karly got worried and hurriedly hid Lily to protect her." Daniel sighed. "I'm sure there are other options, but those are the ones that make the most sense."

"Any chance Lily saw the person who ultimately killed Karly?" Logan asked.

Everyone froze.

Annie's gaze shot to her daughter. "You think she *did* see something and that's why she's not talking?" she whispered.

"I think it's a good possibility." Logan's low tone sent a shiver down her spine.

"Selective mutism due to trauma." Annie's heart dropped to her toes. "I can't ask. I can't push her. Not yet. Besides, it won't do any good. She won't speak. Not until she feels safe." Annie just wanted it all to go away. She wanted her daughter back.

Daniel squeezed her hand. "We'll help in any way we can to bring her back to you."

She had no idea how she would've survived yesterday without him. He'd been her lifeline during her time in Rollins as a teen. And now, again returning as an adult. The man held her heart. Always had. She never understood why he quit writing to her so quickly after she moved. But she took the hint and had walked away from the only love she'd ever known.

Annie half listened to the conversation swirling around her. The trio tossed out ideas and names. She had no more suggestions, so she let them brainstorm. The fear on Lily's face when they found her haunted her mind. What had her little girl gone through? And how did she help Lily recover? Annie knew how to treat physical wounds. Emotional ones? Not so much.

A faint whisper floated across the room. "Good doggy."

She jerked her gaze to Lily. Her daughter was still half asleep, but she'd spoken. Granted it seemed to be subconsciously and directed at Shadow, but Lily had said the words out loud. She looked at Daniel, then Logan and Izzie. "She spoke."

Logan gave her a quiet smile and kept his voice low. "She trusts Shadow. That's the bridge."

Daniel nodded, locking eyes with Annie. "She'll come back to you. It'll just take time."

Annie resisted the urge to scoop her daughter into her arms and rain kisses over her face. Instead, tears streaming down her cheeks, she remained focused on Daniel.

"I'll stand by your side, protect you, and help Lily recover. I promise." Daniel's voice hitched. She watched his Adam's apple bob.

For a heartbeat, the world narrowed to just the two of them. Old memories surfaced, tangling with the present.

Daniel cleared his throat, breaking the link tugging them together. "You and Lily should stay here at the ranch. Until we sort this out."

"Are you sure your mom will be okay with that?" She loved Miss Hannah, but she didn't want to impose or bring danger to the ranch.

"Are you kidding? She lives for taking care of her kids." Daniel pinned her with caring eyes. "And even though you weren't in Rollins long, you are one of hers. Besides, Stone Creek Ranch is safe and secure."

Emotion clogged Annie's throat. All she ever wanted was to be accepted and loved. Besides, she didn't want to be alone, so she didn't hesitate to agree with his offer. "Thank you."

Logan stood. "I'll check the perimeter one more time. Shadow, stay." The dog lifted his snout and tilted his head but didn't move from Lily's side. Logan smiled. "I had a feeling you didn't plan on going anywhere, you crazy mutt."

"While Logan takes care of that, I'm calling the office. We'll find out who killed Bonner and Karly and attacked you. We're not giving whoever this person or people are a second chance to hurt anyone else."

Annie watched the couple leave the room then shifted her gaze to Daniel.

He clasped her hands. "You don't have to do this alone anymore."

"I just want Lily safe."

He nodded. "Then we'll make sure she is. No matter what it takes."

And this time, he meant it with everything he had left in him.

SIX

"Are you sure?" Annie clutched her cell phone, pressing it to her ear. She hadn't wanted to leave Lily this morning, not after last night, but with the fair in full swing and the rodeo a couple days away, she had to come to her office and clean up from the break-in, along with familiarize herself with the small clinic. The struggle between her hurting mother's heart and the reality of keeping her job to be able to support them was real.

"I promise we're doing fine. Shadow is living up to his name. That dog won't let Lily out of his sight." Hannah Sinclair had graciously offered to keep Lily on the ranch. The woman had raised four wonderful children and included her family's friends as her own. From Annie's experience, no one crossed the woman, and if they did, they risked a full-on momma bear moment.

She trusted Miss Hannah and the ranch security, but walking out the door this morning had ripped her heart out. "Thank you. Please give Shadow extra head scratches for me."

"That I can do. Go. Get your work done so you can come home to your daughter. You know I'll take good care of her."

"I do." Annie closed her eyes. "I'll go now. But don't be surprised if I call again."

Hannah laughed. "As if there were any doubt. Goodbye, sweet girl." The line went dead.

She took a deep breath and ran her gaze over the remainder of the mess in her new office. Time to get to work and finish the task.

Annie lifted her hair and fanned her neck. "It's too hot in here." She moved to the opposite wall and kicked the air conditioner down a couple degrees. Cool air blew from the vents. "That's better." Great, she was talking to herself.

The door squeaked open. "Knock, knock."

Annie's attention jerked to the door, where the rodeo director held his cowboy hat in his hands. "Mr. Keats."

"Please, call me Donovan. I'm sorry this is how you were greeted." He waved at the now partially cleaned-up mess. "I hope it doesn't deter you from staying."

Being strong wasn't all it was cracked up to be. For as long as she could remember, she hadn't had a choice. Jumping from one difficult moment in life to another—exhausting. But now? The temptation to grab Lily and run away, escape everything in her life and start over was almost too much to ignore. But if she chose to leave, she'd lose the best support system she'd ever had—Daniel and his family. Something she hadn't experienced with her mom or her ex-boyfriend. Only her time with Daniel as a teen had given her a safe place. So, no. She wouldn't run. "I have no intention of leaving."

"Good." Donovan strolled in and scooped up the last of the papers off the floor and handed them to her. "Since we missed our meeting yesterday, I thought we could discuss your position."

"Of course. Do you mind if I keep working so I can get these documents filed? I hate having medical records out in the open."

Donovan waved at the neat stacks on her desk. "Please, go right ahead." He lowered onto the leather sofa and clasped his hands between his knees. "We've been without an on-site doctor for a couple of months. I'm glad you accepted. This is *your* office. Run it as you see fit. I nor the rodeo board will interfere with your decisions unless they are unlawful or hurt our participants. However, I don't see that happening."

"I can promise you I will adhere to the best medical practices." She understood his warning. He only intended to look out for those under the umbrella of his responsibility.

"Good. I hadn't thought differently but had to say it. If there are any supplies you believe necessary that you don't have, please let me know, and I'll take care of it. After our rodeo weekend, I'll take more time to show you the supply order form and the budget."

"I haven't assessed everything, but at first glance the examination room appears well stocked. Even after someone trashed the building."

"I *am* sorry about that." He gave her a sad smile.

"It's not your fault." Now that she'd met the man in person, she firmly believed that.

He slapped his thighs and stood. "Is there anything else?"

Annie remembered the discussion from last night about her location. "Donovan, did anyone else know about me besides you? Like the person who filed the paperwork?"

"After you told me your situation and why you wanted to come back to Rollins, I thought it was in everyone's best interest to keep it to myself. You had valid reasons for staying under the radar, so to speak. Because of that, I filed the paperwork and announced your acceptance of the job the night before you arrived. No one except me knew you'd been hired before that."

Well, that answered that question. "I'd appreciate it if you continued to keep the reason behind my hire quiet."

"That I can do." His eyes softened. "And if there's anything you need, please, let me know."

"I will. Thank you." Annie's shoulders sagged in relief.

"I'll let you get to it." Donovan left her to finish her task.

A little while later, the files back in place and the exam room tidied, the office phone rang. "Dr. Davis."

"Annie. How's it going?"

"Daniel? Where are you? Why aren't you calling my cell phone?"

"Well, I tried, but you didn't answer." A touch of concern laced his tone.

What? "I don't understand. My phone battery was super low since I forgot to charge it after all the stress last night. I plugged it in over thirty minutes ago." She moved to where she'd placed her phone and checked it. Yup, dead. How? Tracing the cord, she closed her eyes. "The connection isn't completely plugged in. It wasn't charging." Guilt stabbed her. She'd let her line of communication with her daughter die. What if Hannah had needed to get a hold of her and Annie hadn't been in her office? She shook off the internal scolding and made sure she secured the cord. She plopped into her office chair. "Sorry about that."

"It's not a problem. I was just worried when you didn't answer."

"I'm fine, and I talked to your mom before my phone battery went dead, and Lily is safe."

"As if I expected anything different. It is my *mom* we are talking about here."

She chuckled. "Yeah. She is a forced to be reckoned with." The woman was the main reason Annie left Lily at the ranch. Well, that and she didn't want her daughter anywhere near the fairgrounds or carnival. "Since you're playing deputy this morning, have you discovered anything new?"

Daniel gasped. "Playing deputy?" Amusement danced in his voice.

The image of the man slapping a hand on his chest had her rolling her eyes. "You know what I mean."

"Yeah, yeah. Whatever," he teased. His heavy sigh filled

the line. "Unfortunately, we don't have anything new. Deputy McGregor is viewing the security video from yesterday for a second time."

"I hope they find something—anything." Annie twisted the phone cord around her finger, wondering what she'd do if the case stalled.

"We'll do our best to find the man who attacked you and the person who killed Karly."

Daniel and Izzie would. She knew that. But she couldn't keep the nagging fear flickering inside her at bay. They had a list of possible suspects, but no one stood out. That reminded her. "By the way, Donovan Keats came by this morning."

"What did he have to say?" Daniel didn't sound worried. Only curious.

"We went over the job—mostly. I did ask about who filed my paperwork."

"And?"

"He did it. I had shared the basics with Donovan, and he took my situation very seriously."

"So, he knows why you came here?"

"Yes. To a degree. I couldn't lie when he asked me why I wanted a job that travels at times since I had a four-year-old." Annie rubbed her forehead. "I'm sure you need to get back to work, and I plan to head out and mentally map out the arena. I don't want to go into the rodeo this weekend clueless."

He chuckled. "I can understand that. If I need you and your phone is still charging, I'll call the landline in your office or go old school and leave you a note on stone tablets or something. Maybe I'll resort to skywriting."

She rolled her eyes at his ridiculousness. "That'll work."

"Annie."

"Yeah?"

"Be careful out there." The worry in Daniel's tone did funny things to her heart.

"I will." Her words came out as a whisper. She hung up. Her gaze traveled her new office. Except for the threats to her and Lily, the new job might be the break she needed from the high-octane emergency department that had been her life for the past several years. Maybe she'd hold off applying to Rollins General Hospital for a bit and enjoy the slower pace of work.

Time to inspect where she'd hang out at the rodeos, watching and waiting in case the participants required her medical talents.

She confirmed that the file cabinets and exam room were locked and left the building. The scent of hay, horses, and other animals filled her senses. Her boots kicked up dirt as she made her way to the arena. Amazing how sweet memories could calm her nerves.

Cowboys and cowgirls waved. Some approached her, welcoming her to Rollins, and asked about Lily. She'd missed the instant comradery of a small town and the rodeo community. Not that she ever competed. But she'd spent a few summers here at the rodeo grounds, hanging out with friends—and Daniel. The place had changed—updated and expanded. Entering the arena, she studied the chutes and gates. Then her attention shifted to the ingress and egress for medical emergencies. Not too bad. Whoever had designed the new layout had done a good job.

She glanced at her watch. Time to return to her office and call the fire department and ask about response time. She'd already discovered that any major trauma would either reroute to Lackard or the patient had to wait on a trauma doctor to make the trip to Rollins. Not a great situation, but with her experience and Lackard only forty minutes or so away it would do.

A few minutes later, she strode into her office. Her phone showed a 60 percent charge. At least she could take it with her next time she left the building. Her gaze landed on her desk. A note sat in the center.

Annie, I found something. Come join me at the fairground outbuildings. I'm in the one that holds the portable fencing and signs.
—Daniel

A burst of hope filled her. She tucked the note in her pocket, grabbed her cell phone, and hurried out the door.

Please let him have found answers to this nonsense.

She rounded the barns and headed to the storage buildings at the far end of the fairgrounds. She slowed and looked around. No one appeared to be there. "Daniel?"

No answer.

She checked her cell phone for a message. Nothing. She stepped closer to the shed and peeked inside. Turning on her phone flashlight app, she scanned the interior. Tables lay stacked against one wall. Sandwich signs rested against the other side. Everything appeared quiet. Where was he? Isn't this where he said to join him?

A hand struck her back and shoved her inside. The cell phone flew from her hand, clattering on the concrete floor, ricocheted off a metal pole, and bounced outside. She landed on her hands and knees. Pain from the hard landing sliced through her limbs. The door slammed shut and darkness surrounded her. The distinct click of the lock sent panic rippling through her.

Realization set in. Daniel hadn't left her the note. Her attacker had. Tears pricked her eyes. How soon would someone find her? Unless her attacker had kicked her phone away or picked it up, maybe she could wiggle her fingers under the door and fish for it.

A light hiss from the corner of the building sent shivers down her spine. Her imagination ran wild with the possibilities. A snake? Another animal? Her body convulsed at the idea of being unable to escape.

Come on, Annie, calm down and think.

After a few deep breaths, Annie stood and took a step toward her only option—the faint outline of the door. Her head swirled. She grabbed on to the nearest object to steady herself. A folded table standing on end. Unable to stay upright, she leaned into it and toppled to the floor.

What was wrong with her?

A moment of clarity struck. The slow hiss—a gas of some sort—aimed to kill her.

She closed her eyes, willing down the bile creeping up her throat. If she controlled her breathing and moved away from the hissing, she'd gain precious moments, allowing Daniel time to find her.

Struggling to her hands and knees, she crawled toward the opposite corner closest to the door, praying fresh air would seep through the cracks. She collapsed and curled into the fetal position. Tears rolled down her temples and dripped onto the dirty floor.

God, help. But whatever happens to me, protect Lily.

A burst of hot breeze whipped across Daniel's face. The temperatures had risen a smidge, but the humidity had skyrocketed. He lifted his cowboy hat and wiped his brow. The latest bit of information on the case hadn't helped him discover the masked man's identity or who had killed Karly. He was no closer to solving the case or cases. Which? He wasn't sure. Unease had settled into his bones a few minutes ago, spurring him to check on Annie. Knowing she hadn't had her phone with her when she'd checked out the arena egged him to walk faster to the medical clinic.

Opening the door, he called out.

Silence met his ears.

"Annie?" He peeked into the exam room. Not in there either. Checking her desk, he noticed her cell phone missing.

She must have returned, grabbed it, and left again. He dialed her number. The phone rang. When it went to voicemail, he clicked it off. "Where are you?"

Nothing appeared out of place. He dialed his mom.

"Hey, son."

"Hi, Mom. Has Annie called recently?" He took in the room with a law enforcement eye.

"Not since earlier this morning. Why? What's wrong?"

"I'm not sure. She's not in her office and isn't answering her phone."

"I can understand not being in her office, but not picking up a call doesn't sound like her. Especially after the incidents with Lily. But you also know how that fairground can be. The rodeo grounds have decent service. The fairgrounds—not so much."

"Same at the carnival. And the noise doesn't help." He released a long slow breath. "You're right. I'm overreacting."

"I'm not saying that." His mom paused for a moment. "Trust your gut, honey. If her absence is bothering you, then go search for her."

As always, his mom was right. His gut told him to find her. "Thanks, Mom. Love you."

"Love you too, sweet boy." His mother hung up.

He placed a call to Izzie.

"Sheriff Sinclair." His sister sounded distracted.

"Hey, sis."

"Daniel. What's going on?"

"Annie's not in her office, and I've got a bad feeling about it."

"Meet me at the entrance of the horse barn. We'll ask around and see if we can track down the last person to see her and where."

"See you soon." He stuffed his phone in his pocket and strode out the door. His objective? To find Annie—and fast.

His spidey senses were tingling. And nothing good ever came from that.

The familiar scent of the horse barn swirled in the air. Daniel spotted his sister and angled toward her.

"Anything?"

He shook his head. "She's not answering her phone, and I don't like it."

"Are you sure she has it?" Izzie widened her stance and folded her arms, looking like the no-nonsense sheriff she was.

"Not one hundred percent. It died earlier by accident. She plugged it in and told me she planned to go to the arena. When I stopped by her office a few minutes ago, she and her phone were missing. I called Mom. She hasn't heard from Annie lately, but Lily's fine."

The creases in Izzie's forehead deepened. "I agree. Something's off. I'll have Logan check on Lily just to make sure. You go toward the fairgrounds. See if anyone has seen her. I'll do a loop through the rodeo grounds and meet you by the storage buildings on the far side."

"Sounds like a plan." Daniel threw up a prayer of thanks for his sister's help and one for Annie's safety.

Ten minutes and some twenty people later, Daniel rounded the final animal barn and headed in the direction of the storage sheds. The back area was blocked off from the public and deserted. A handful of 4-H members had seen Annie hurrying in this direction. What had brought her out here? And where was she?

He stopped in the middle of the gravel circle. Weeds sprouted between the rocks in small patches. None appeared to have been recently smashed down by vehicles. However… He moved closer to the buildings the county used for fair storage. Daniel crouched and examined the ground. Fresh footprints marred the otherwise uncut grass. Odd. Maybe one of the youth leaders forgot some supplies. A weird occurrence since the fair started a few days ago. But not impossible.

Daniel stood and studied the area. The sun reflected off a piece of glass, tugging him to investigate the far building. With cautious steps, he moved closer to the locked shed. A cell phone lay face up. He tapped the screen. Lily's smiling face filled the display. Annie's.

"Annie!" He spun in a slow circle. Where was she?

"Yo, Daniel. You find anything?" Izzie strode toward him.

He held up the phone. "Annie's, but she's nowhere in sight."

"You go that way." His sister pointed to the far side of the storage buildings. "I'll go the other way. Look for any evidence to point us to where she might be. Meet you behind the sheds."

"Got it." Daniel scrutinized every bent weed. Every scuffed section of the ground. When he rounded the back corner of the building, he spotted a CO2 tank from a soda machine sitting near the shed. A tube ran up the wall and disappeared through a tiny gap near the roofline. His lungs seized. "Izzie!"

He hurried to the tank and shut off the valve, then sprinted to the front and yanked on the door. But it didn't budge. He muttered to himself about being stupid and not using his brain. Of course it wouldn't open, the shed was locked.

Izzie ran to meet him. "What'd you find?"

"A soda machine tank around back pumping CO2 into a tube that feeds into the building. Annie has to be in here."

"Don't jump to conclusions." Izzie might have warned him, but she pulled a key ring from her pocket. "I have the master key for all the park buildings. Move over." His sister unlocked the door and unholstered her weapon. She stood off center of the doorway, gun and flashlight at the ready.

Daniel nodded, opened the door, and moved to the side with his Sig Sauer in hand ready to back his sister up.

Izzie lifted her hands. The flashlight illuminating the interior, she moved forward into the small building. Professional and swift. "Daniel, get in here!"

Izzie's panicked tone had him racing inside.

Annie lay unconscious on the ground. His stomach in his throat, he holstered his weapon, then scooped her up and rushed outside into the fresh air. He laid her on the ground and knelt next to her. His finger shook as he placed them against her neck to feel for a pulse. "Come on. Come on."

"Settle down, bro." Izzie towered over him.

He took in a lung full of air and pushed it out through pursed lips. He tried again. Steadier this time, his fingers found the faint thump against her skin. "She's alive."

"I'll call for the paramedics."

"Annie. Can you hear me?" He brushed the sweaty hair from her forehead. "Please, wake up."

Her stillness made his heart race. Had he been too late? Had he found her again, only to lose her? Through the years, he'd never gotten involved with another woman. Oh, he'd gone on dates. Even had a couple of girlfriends for a short time, but neither relationship lasted. Now he knew why. His heart had been waiting for Annie to return. He never wanted to let her go.

And what about Lily? She'd almost lost another mom. Lily. Another problem standing in his way of a future with Annie. Oh, the little girl was sweet and as cute as could be, but trusting himself with a child? Could he do that? Even for the woman who'd claimed his heart as a teen?

The medic unit drove into the gravel circle and came to a stop. Tanner and Brady grabbed their equipment and hurried over.

Daniel went straight into work mode. He might be a mess inside, but he refused to waste time. Annie's life depended on everyone doing their job. "Thirty-year-old female. Apparent hypoxia due to CO2 inhalation."

Tanner dropped beside him and prepped the oxygen tank

and tubing. "How long?" The man's practiced skills had an oxygen mask over Annie's nose and mouth in less than a minute.

"Uncertain. Twenty, thirty minutes maybe." Daniel had no idea, but if he backtracked the timeline, that was his best guess.

"I'm hoping for the twenty," Brady mumbled.

Yeah, me too, buddy. Me too. Daniel knew enough about hypoxia that those ten minutes could make all the difference between a full recovery and… He refused to finish that thought.

With the oxygen flowing, the medics focused on her vitals.

Daniel held her limp hand and brushed his thumb back and forth across her pale skin. A hand rested on his shoulder. He glanced up into Izzie's sympathetic gaze. Tears pricked his eyes. He blinked to keep them from falling. Regrets of leaving her this morning barreled into him. Blame over not putting security outside her office made his stomach churn. But it was the possibility of not making it in time to save her that washed over him like a tsunami. He refocused on the woman he'd dreamed about for years.

Her eyelids fluttered but didn't open.

"Come on, Annie. Wake up," Daniel whispered.

Izzie squeezed his shoulder. The woman was as fierce as they came when it came to family, but her touch gave him a sense of strength. Just knowing she was there helped.

The common fair and carnival noises faded into the background. The beat of his heart pounded his chest. Brady and Tanner worked as a team without words. It was as if everyone was too afraid to speak.

Annie's hand twitched. He laced his fingers with hers and prayed. Like everything else in life, God was in control. Although Daniel would admit that he didn't always like the Big Guy's decisions.

A cough jerked his gaze to her face. She coughed again. Her eyes opened and slammed shut.

Daniel leaned over into her line of vision. "Hey, welcome back. Did you have a good nap?" He didn't feel like it, but he grinned.

She squinted, and her forehead scrunched.

He adjusted his angle, blocking out the sun. "Better?"

The relief in her features was immediate. "Thanks." Her words slurred.

A quick glance at Tanner's relieved smile had Daniel releasing the pent-up tension that had built since he'd discovered Annie missing.

"Hi, Annie. Name's Brady. Nice to see you again." The paramedic monitored her vitals while he spoke. "Can you tell me your full name and what month it is?"

Eyes closed, she swallowed. "Anderson Davis. Always gone by Annie. And it's August. I think. Foggy."

Brady flashed the penlight in her eyes, checking her pupils. "Looks like as soon as we clear your system with oxygen, you'll be good to go. How about something for that headache?"

A smile tugged at the corner of Annie's mouth. "I could kiss you for that suggestion."

Daniel gritted his teeth.

"Easy, bro. It was a figure of speech." Amusement danced in Izzie's tone.

Daniel resisted the urge to turn around and smack her. The woman was his sister after all. Albeit his annoying sister, but she was right about his reaction. However, he'd never give her the satisfaction of telling her that.

Feelings he'd buried since Annie had moved away resurfaced. He wouldn't deny it any longer. How could he? Annie had become the measure for every woman he'd dated. And none compared. His heart wanted her.

Her near-death experience had shaken him. And he must have lost his mind in the process. Why else would he not care that she had a daughter when children were his kryptonite?

Daniel cupped her cheek, avoiding the oxygen mask. "Let's get you to the hospital then back to the ranch so you can recover."

She leaned into his touch and closed her eyes.

For the first time in years, his world settled. No longer tilted at an odd angle but perfectly situated on its axis.

"We'll get your statement later. But I promise we'll find out who is threatening you and put a stop to it." There he went making promises he might not be able to keep. But he'd die trying if it meant Annie's safety.

SEVEN

The hardwood floor creaked under Annie's feet. A sweet cinnamon aroma drifted from the kitchen. She'd spent several hours at the hospital before Daniel whisked her away to Stone Creek Ranch. He'd hovered over her since he found her locked in the small storage building. From what he'd told her, her attacker had threaded a tube through an opening and pumped in carbon dioxide from a soda machine tank. She had God to thank that the tube kinked and slowed the flow. Otherwise, she'd be dead instead of craving the mouthwatering breakfast that awaited her.

A dull headache had settled in, and she remained a bit sluggish, but overall, the oxygen had done its job. She padded into the kitchen and came to a halt.

Lily sat on the floor, legs crisscrossed, using the chair seat as a table while Shadow lay with his head in her lap. Cheeks full of cinnamon roll, she stroked the dog's head. No doubt adding sticky sugar to the poor animal's fur.

Annie leaned against the doorframe and smiled. "I see someone is feeding you sweets."

Her daughter's eyes lifted. The hollowness in her gaze stole Annie's breath. Lily returned her attention to the cut up cinnamon roll on her plate and stuffed another piece into her mouth.

Tears bubbled to the surface. Lily had lost her zest for life.

The only person—dog—thing? Whatever you wanted to call it. Shadow was the only one who'd reached her so far. And that made Annie's mom-heart hurt.

"Sorry about that." Daniel's deep timbre yanked her from her thoughts. He sat on the other side of the table as if scared to sit beside Lily.

"About what?"

He gestured to the pastry. "I didn't think about you not wanting her to have it."

Lily's eyes darted between her and Daniel as if watching a drama on TV.

Annie pushed from the door. "No. It's fine. We have donuts and such from time to time. It's not like she can't have sugar. Besides, I think she deserves extra treats after the past few days."

The hint of a smile tugged at her daughter's lips but fell as quickly as it had started. The little girl gripped Shadow's fur in her tiny hand. The dog had become Lily's lifeline. How had Annie and Lily's life gone so far off course?

"Good. I'm glad I didn't overstep. Mom makes the best cinnamon rolls."

"I remember."

Daniel stood. "Have a seat. I'll get you a plate and some coffee."

"I appreciate that." Even after a full night's sleep, fatigue had wrapped around her like a weighted blanket. She knew the medical cause and the recovery, but that didn't mean it wasn't frustrating. Annie sat next to her daughter and placed her hand on the top of the girl's head. She probably needed the connection more than Lily did.

Her daughter glanced up but continued to eat and pet Shadow.

Maybe once things settled down, she should consider getting Lily a dog. A plate and mug appeared before her. Blinking away her trailing thoughts, she dug into the cinnamon roll. If it were possible, her eyes would have rolled back into her head. She groaned at the deliciousness of Hannah Sinclair's baking abilities. "Better than I remember."

Daniel chuckled behind his coffee mug. "Mom does have a way with food."

She nodded and finished her breakfast in silence. However, she'd noticed Daniel's gaze land on Lily multiple times. The unease in his demeanor wasn't hard to miss. It went beyond the recent events. What happened to cause his reaction to her daughter? Her mind went to her ex, Ethan, and how he'd brushed her off when Lily's presence in her life got in the way. Never again. Friends or more, it didn't matter. She and her daughter came as a package deal.

Fatigue might have its claws in her, but since her brushes with death, her attitude had changed. No longer willing to push things aside, she placed her cup on the table and pinned him with her gaze. "Could we talk—in private?"

He jerked at her no-nonsense words. "Of course. But what about..." He gestured toward Lily.

Annie didn't want to leave her alone, but she had to clear the air. "Is anyone in the house?"

"Logan's working in the office. Let me ask him to come watch her for a bit." He scooted his chair out and strode from the kitchen.

"Lily, Momma needs to have a chat with Mr. Daniel. Mr. Logan's going to come hang out with you and Shadow. He's the one letting you borrow his dog."

Her daughter's gaze lifted, then she continued to snuggle with Shadow while she finished eating. Lily hadn't uttered a single word since they'd heard her talking to the dog.

Annie missed her little chatterbox. The entire event had escalated her stress level to mountaintop heights, but the selective mutism had shattered her heart.

Finished with her breakfast, Lily scrambled to her feet and put the plate on the counter. Shadow trotted behind, staying within reach of his charge. Annie followed and wetted a couple of paper towels. "Let's get you cleaned up so you don't get that sticky mess all over Miss Hannah's house."

Lily held out her hands and lifted her face. Her daughter didn't appear scared, just chose not to speak.

God, how do I reach her? What happened to make her stop talking?

"All done. Why don't you and Shadow go to the living room? I believe Miss Hannah left the toys in there for you."

Without further encouragement, Lily patted the dog's head and wandered into the living room with Shadow following behind her.

Annie grinned. Shadow. A perfect name for the sweet black Lab.

The pair plopped onto the floor, and Lily pulled stuffed animals from the basket. The child was not a doll girl. Give her a stuffy, building blocks, and coloring books any day.

She took the moment to watch her daughter. Warmth filled her chest. She could have so easily lost her precious baby.

"Hey, Lily." Logan strode into the room. "Mind if I stay with you while your mom talks with Daniel?"

Eyes on the plush bear, Lily shrugged.

Annie's eyebrows shot up. She jerked her gaze to Logan. Lily hadn't responded to anyone's questions before now.

He mouthed, *Wow.*

"Thank you for chillin' with Lily. I'll be right outside on the porch if you need me."

"We'll be fine. Won't we, Lily?" Logan sat on the recliner and opened his laptop. "I plan to work while Lily and Shadow build something cool."

Her daughter didn't respond that time, but Annie was grateful for Logan's attempt.

"Go on. We'll be fine." The man gave a little wave and focused on his work.

Annie nodded and slipped onto the porch.

Daniel stood, hands in his pockets, staring out across his family's ranch.

She joined him at the white-painted wooden railing. The sun had turned on the heat. Even in the morning hours the temps had shot up, along with the humidity. Sweat had begun to bead on her upper lip. But the birds chirping in the trees and the wildflowers dotting the pasture beyond the backyard made up for the uncomfortable weather. Here—on the ranch—she felt safe. Daniel and Logan had discussed the security measures with her soon after she'd first arrived. It was the reason she'd left Lily on the ranch while she and Daniel had gone to the rodeo grounds yesterday.

"You wanted to talk?" The seriousness of his tone was an unfamiliar sound. The man tended to joke about everything.

"I…um…" How did she go about asking him what his problem was with her daughter?

He shifted. His eyes met hers. If it were possible, she would have melted under his tender gaze. "I've missed you."

Annie's fingers found their way to his arm. The simple touch grounded her and chased away her fears. The boy—now man—had always had that effect on her. His caring and kindness had drawn her to him all those years ago. And the fact he was easy on the eyes hadn't gone unnoticed either. But looks don't make the man—actions do. And Daniel's actions now and when she'd left Rollins spoke volumes, but she couldn't deny her feelings.

"And I've missed you. I wish we wouldn't have allowed distance to come between us." She'd wondered so many times how her life would have turned out differently.

The crease in his forehead deepened. "*You* wish?"

"Yeah. I wrote you so many times, but you stopped answering my emails." She thought they'd had something special, but apparently, he hadn't felt that way.

"*I* stopped?" He looked at her like she had three heads and a tail.

"What is wrong with you? You're turning my comments into weird questions."

"Because I wrote you over a dozen times with no response. *You* ghosted *me*."

She straightened her shoulders. How dare he put that on her. "I absolutely did not."

"Annie, I wrote you two or three times a week. I received emails back from you for the first few months, then you stopped writing. I kept trying, but after a couple of months of not hearing from you, I assumed you'd moved on and forgot all about me."

Her jaw dropped open. How had that happened? Then it hit her. Her mother. The woman had made her life miserable for as long as she could remember. Anytime Annie had made a good friend, her mother had sabotaged the relationship in some way or another. "My mother. I wasn't allowed a cell phone, and we shared a computer. She had access to my account. She must have set up notification alerts and intercepted and deleted our emails before either of us saw them. She hated that we'd become close. Blamed me for the reason we moved."

"Why would she do that?" Daniel tilted his head. "I don't understand."

Life had never been easy for Annie. But her mother's betrayal stung. The woman had taken the only good thing in Annie's world and cut it out like removing a tumor. She exhaled, then spun away from Daniel's gaze and grabbed the rail. "Mom was..." How did she describe the woman? "For as long as I can remember, she wasn't a happy person. Always grasping for love with the first man to pay attention to her. It never worked out. She was too needy. Too desperate. After a short time, the men would walk away, leaving her lonely and angry. She wasn't a nice person during those times."

Daniel moved next to her and mimicked her stance. "Did she hurt you? You know, physically?"

She shrugged. "I was on the receiving end of a few backhands, but in general, Mom was more emotionally abusive than anything else." Annie focused on a small yellow flower swaying in the light breeze. "No. That's not right either. It was more like she wished I didn't exist and ignored me."

"That still doesn't explain why she kept us apart."

"I think our relationship made her jealous. It's the only thing that makes sense."

"I'm sorry I thought the worst."

She shifted to face him. "I wasn't any better. I assumed you found another girl and didn't care anymore."

His eyes softened. "I never stopped caring about you after you left. Even when I thought you were gone for good."

Annie blinked away the tears threatening to fall. "I didn't want to go, but Mom made me, and then she kept me from you." The lump in her throat grew. "I didn't forget you either."

Silence filled the air. Their eyes locked on to each other. Unspoken words passed between them.

Daniel cleared his throat. "Tell me about what happened during those missing years."

They had gotten so far off track of why she'd brought him out here to talk, but with the realization of her mother's awful action, she'd back away from confronting him about his uneasiness around Lily and fill in the blanks of their missing years. Maybe if she opened up, he'd answer her questions without sensor.

She gestured toward the porch swing and lowered herself onto the bench.

"The ranch should be safe, but with you out here in the open, I refuse to risk it. Let me check in with Garrett and ensure the critter cams haven't picked up unwanted movement. Then I'm all yours." He stood at the rail and focused on his phone. Ever the protector.

Her gaze raked over the property, wondering if complacency would be her downfall. But the ranch had always been her sanctuary. Her shelter from the storms of life. God had given her refuge among this family and on this land. Then and now.

Danger lurked beyond the tree-lined perimeter, but right or wrong, the cocoon of the ranch gave her a sense of peace.

Daniel tucked his phone away and joined her on the seat. He pushed them into motion.

Memories swarmed her thoughts. The way they'd sit out here in the evenings before she'd go home to an unwelcoming house. Back then, she'd wish for the day to never end.

She took a deep breath. "Things didn't change much when we moved to Houston. Mom seemed to have erased all evidence of us living in Rollins. I have no idea why, and probably never will. Everyone assumed we moved from the previous town we'd lived in—Mom's hometown. I kept my head down at school and got good grades. Enough that I was granted a full ride scholarship to one of the universities in Houston. I moved out that fall to attend college and never looked back." She hadn't seen or heard from her mother since the day she packed the car that she'd purchased on her own and drove off. Granted, Annie hadn't tried either, but it still hurt that the woman who should have loved her unconditionally never reached out—not once. "Again, I worked hard and graduated early with my bachelor's degree. I immediately went to medical school on grants and a few student loans. Countless hours of schoolwork and hospital rotations later—poof, I was a doctor."

Daniel chuckled. "Somehow, I don't think it was that easy, but go ahead—continue."

"You're right. Some days I asked myself why. But once I found a position as an emergency medical physician in San Antonio it all became clear. I loved what I did. All the years of putting up with Mom's hatred vanished. I had friends and a purpose. Life seemed perfect, except for one thing."

"And what was that?"

"You," she whispered.

The swing jerked to a stop. "Me?"

"I missed you. I often wondered what happened to you. If you were happy." If he'd married and had kids. She mentally rolled her eyes. Nope, she wouldn't say that.

He bowed his head. "I wish I would have known you weren't ghosting me. I'd have figured out a way to contact you."

Her heart swelled, knowing the man beside her hadn't walked away on purpose.

Daniel pushed the swing into motion. "Go on. Tell me more. I want to know everything." His fingers brushed her hair. Then as if he realized what he'd done, he dropped his hand.

"I met a man—another doctor, Ethan Galin. I thought we had something. I thought I'd found the love I'd been missing my entire life. We talked about getting married and joining Doctors Without Borders. Working in remote areas of the world together. But plans changed."

Daniel laced his fingers with hers, giving her support to get through the reality of what happened.

"My best friend, Libby, and her husband were in a car accident. The paramedics rushed them to the emergency department in the hospital where I worked. I happened to be on duty that night."

"Oh, Annie. I'm so sorry." Daniel's empathetic gaze about took her to the ground.

"It gets worse." She sucked in a breath. "I was the specialist for her injuries. I tried to recuse myself because of our relationship, but a replacement physician wasn't a viable option. She needed surgery immediately. So, I was the one who treated her. I was the one who couldn't save her. She died on the operating table. The nurses hadn't told me until I came from the surgery that her husband had died on the way to the hospital. It was a rare date night for them. They had busy lives and a one-year-old at home. The week after Lily was born, Libby added my name to their living trust as her child's legal guardian. I agreed, never believing for a moment that I'd have to accept that responsibility. But that night changed everything." Annie wiped the tears sneaking down her cheeks. "When Ethan continued to talk about our dream of working overseas, I refused to leave Lily. And I couldn't take her with me. Can you imagine a one-year-old in the depths of a developing country with a parent who worked sixteen-hour days? I couldn't do it. I owed it to Libby to keep her daughter. And once I held her in my arms, I knew I'd never let her go."

"You didn't follow your dream of Doctors Without Borders." Daniel rubbed his thumb over the back of her hand.

"You know, I'm not sure it was ever my dream. I think I fell in love with the fact that I had a partner."

"What happened to Ethan?"

"I told him I couldn't go because of Lily." She swallowed the boulder-sized lump that had formed in her throat. "He didn't care. He went ahead and signed up. When they called him to join, he left me without a second thought." She'd been nothing to him, just like her mother.

"I'm so sorry, Annie." Daniel wrapped her in his arms and held her close.

"You'd think I'd be used to it, being treated that way, but I'd hoped he was different." She hiccupped a sob. "He wasn't. But I had Lily, who'd lost her parents and needed me. I refused to let her grow up feeling like an intrusion in my life. She deserves better than that."

"Did you have help?"

"Yes and no. I had my church family, but it was awkward. Young single professionals made up the group that I attended. No married couples and no children. They weren't much help in that manner, but they did support me."

"I'm glad you had someone."

"Me too." Her church group had thrown her a baby shower and took turns bringing her meals for the first couple of months. A few offered to babysit as well. They tried. But loneliness had set in. She had no one to turn to for advice. And her hours at the hospital about did her in, but she'd survived. She'd eventually found a rhythm to life with a child.

"What about your mom? Did she offered to help?"

A humorless laugh bubbled from Annie. "I haven't seen or talked to her since the day I left for college. She's never once called me. I thought maybe she'd miss me. Boy was I wrong. I gave up hope."

"I wish I could take all your pain away." His hand brushed down her hair. "If it helps, you're a wonderful mom."

Annie sniffed. "It does." Several minutes later, she pulled away. Aware they had a killer to find, but she refused to walk away without knowing why Daniel avoided being around Lily. She'd bared her heart to him. It was time to get answers about his reaction to her daughter. "Daniel, the reason I asked you out here wasn't to spill my life story."

He stiffened as if he knew he wouldn't like what she had to say.

"What do you have against my daughter? Every time you're around her, you keep your distance. Well, as much as possible. You act like she's a rabid animal who'll attack you at any moment."

He jumped from the swing and hurried to the porch railing. Hands on the bar, he bowed his head.

Whatever the reason, it brought the man pain.

She moved next to him and placed her hand on his back. "Please tell me what's wrong."

Could Daniel tell her about his fears and the reasons for them? His eyes traveled across the expanse of the property. The ranch had always been his safe place. That's why he'd brought Annie and Lily here. The security system wasn't state of the art, but he'd put the critter cams dotting the perimeter and the eyes and ears of the ranch hands above any sophisticated system out there. That's why he felt comfortable sitting out in the open on the porch while a killer ran loose in Rollins. But he wouldn't ignore the situation. He'd be vigilant, and he'd continue to check his app and message Garrett for updates.

But to Annie's question, as much as it raised his anxiety to have a child under his protection, he'd done it out of respect and affection for his teenage best friend. The woman who'd never left his thoughts even after he assumed she'd abandoned him. Now, he knew better.

He blew out a long breath. "You noticed that, did you?"

An exasperated huffed escaped her lips. "Of course. It wasn't hard to miss."

"Fair enough." He ran a hand over his face. The truth he'd buried deep had come to the surface. "I've never told anyone what I'm about to tell you."

She grasped his hand and led him back to the swing. "If you trust me with your secret, I won't tell a soul."

He pushed the swing into motion with his toe. The movement eased a bit of the tension but not enough. Anytime the memories got too much, he'd take his horse, Aspen, out and ride for hours. He craved time out in nature with Aspen. He'd even run across the field in his cowboy boots. Anything to avoid this conversation. Not even his go-to—a joke—could eliminate his pain. But this was Annie. His ride or die buddy he'd never forgotten.

"You're right. Lily does make me..." What was the word he wanted to use? "Uneasy. Not due to anything she's done but because of what she represents."

"And what's that?" This time she clasped his hand.

He glanced at her and immediately wished he hadn't. The kindness and concern in her eyes hit him like a dagger to the chest. "Failure. Regret. Helplessness."

"Daniel, what happened?" Annie held his forearm. Her touch grounding him in the present. "Tell me."

Sucking in a shaky breath, he leaned forward and held his head in his hands. "During my field training while I was in the academy, my field officer and I were called to a multiple car accident." He kept his hands over his face as the memory surfaced with brutal clarity. "Three vehicles. The first was a pickup with its grill smashed in almost to the dashboard. The second vehicle had flipped and landed on its roof—crushed so badly I couldn't tell what kind of car it had been. The third was half in the ditch. The sounds and smell..." He shook his head. "The strangely sweet smell of engine fluids, hot rubber from the tires, metal creaking, people screaming. It was chaos."

Annie didn't speak. Just sat quietly beside him, her hand still resting on his forearm, anchoring him.

"My field officer and I ran straight for the overturned car. I don't know why we chose that one. It must have been the screaming. A little boy. He couldn't have been more than four or five. He was trapped in the crumpled metal. I could see his legs through the shattered glass, hear him crying for help. And I couldn't get to him." Daniel's voice cracked. "The passenger side was crushed flat, but I tried pulling at what appeared to be the remains of the door. When that didn't work, I tried breaking the rest of the window. The cries got louder, more frantic. I was desperate to get in. I cut my hands on the glass. I even tried crawling under the wreckage, but my mentor dragged me away and told me to wait on the hydraulic spreader."

Annie's eyes filled with tears, but she stayed quiet, letting him speak.

"By the time the equipment came, it was too late. One minute he was there, and then…gone." He swallowed hard, a tear slipping down his cheek. "And I couldn't do anything. I couldn't save him." He stared at the distant pasture, his voice barely audible. "I've lived with that moment every day since. His voice. That helplessness. That regret. The nightmares won't let go. It's why I panicked when I found out you had a kid. Then when Lily went missing." His heart thundered in his chest. "Deep down I am afraid I'll fail another child. Afraid I'll fail who is the most precious person on earth to you. I can't live with that guilt again. And I wouldn't survive if I let you down."

Annie reached out, placed her palm on his wet cheek, and gently turned his face back toward her. Her own eyes were shining with unshed tears, but her expression held no judgment. Only understanding. "Listening to your story helps me understand why you shied away from Lily. Thank you for telling me. But, Daniel, that little boy's death wasn't your fault."

"It felt like it was. Still does." He'd ran every action, every decision through his mind, but each time the results were the same. A child died because of his inability to save him.

"You did everything you could. You didn't walk away. You didn't give up. That matters." She paused. "God doesn't ask us to save everyone. Only to be faithful with what's in front of us. To do our best and rely on Him."

He stared at her, the weight of her words pressing against the years of regret he'd carried. "I know that. In my head, I know it. But my heart still struggles to believe it."

She gave him a small, sad smile. "Sometimes faith is just choosing to show up—even when the pain tells you to run."

He leaned back, considering her words. The swing creaked

softly as they sat in silence. Daniel exhaled and laced their fingers.

"You've always known how to say the right thing."

"I don't know about that," she whispered. "That's why you've turned into Mr. Funny Man, isn't it."

"According to my family, I've held that title since the day I was born."

Annie shook her head. "It's more now. It's your defense mechanism—a way to keep people from looking too closely—from seeing your pain."

"Maybe." He felt like someone had filleted his heart and left it open for the world to see.

"You're not alone anymore. You don't have to hide the truth any longer." Annie wiped his tear-streaked cheek with the pad of her thumb.

He let her words settle into the broken places. For the first time in years, the hurt didn't cut so deep.

"I don't know if the echoes of that little boy's screams will ever vanish, but thank you for listening. For pushing me to tell you. I feel like a weight has lifted."

"I'm glad I could help."

"You've done more than that. I want the opportunity to see where this goes. But I also know that I'm not healed from that event in my past. So, please be patient with me. I'm willing to try to let go and stop pushing Lily away." Could he do it? Maybe. Maybe not. Only time would tell.

"I'd love that." Annie rested her head on his shoulder.

Me too, Annie. Me too.

Now if he could figure out how to keep the mother-daughter duo safe and find the person responsible for the threats on their life, he might allow himself to dream of a future that included the woman who'd stolen his heart as a teen and her daughter who might possess the key to healing the brokenness inside him.

EIGHT

Dressed in her new work attire, jeans and a short-sleeve shirt, Annie tied her hair into a ponytail and studied her image in the bathroom mirror. She didn't recognize the woman staring back at her. Dark circles marred the skin under her eyes. The past couple of days had deepened the worry lines in her features. No amount of makeup could hide the stress that had taken root. Daniel's heart-to-heart conversation had eased the tension between them, but with the unidentified killer or killers still on the loose, her nerves continued to stretch—ready to snap.

She stared at her reflection. "You can do it, Annie. You're a survivor." *Yeah, right. Barely.* She slapped her hands on the counter and hung her head. *Pull yourself together. You have a job to do and a daughter to think about.* And that was part of the problem. The unease of leaving Lily again at Stone Creek Ranch pressed down heavy on Annie like the Texas humidity, stealing her breath. She had no reason to fear her daughter staying with Miss Hannah and Logan, but the mother in her bristled at saying goodbye and heading to her office. Lily continued to cling to her selective mutism. That worried Annie more than she had let on. She smoothed her hair, double-checked her appearance, and headed for the kitchen.

"Good morning, dear." Hannah poured a cup of coffee and held it out for her.

"Morning, Miss Hannah." Annie accepted the mug.

"She's in the living room with Daniel."

Annie chuckled. "I didn't ask."

"But you were thinking it."

"Well, that's true."

"Don't worry. He'll figure it out." Hannah hung a dish towel on the oven handle.

Annie glanced at the doorway. Figure out what? His issues with Lily?

"Garrett called. He requested my help in the horse barn. Something about a broken gate and needs my approval or some such nonsense. That man is honest to a fault. Why would I question his judgment? It's not like he'd cheat me out of money." Hannah shook her head. "Call me if you need me." The back door clicked shut.

"Well, okay, then. I guess we'll talk later." Annie shook her head. That woman was a force to be reckoned with. Hands wrapped around her cup, she meandered into the living room.

Lily and Shadow sat on a blanket Miss Hannah had spread out on the floor. Toys lay beside them. Her daughter's hand stroked the dog's fur. Daniel lay on his side next to Shadow, talking to the Lab. Lily appeared half interested in the conversation.

"Right, Shadow?" Daniel asked.

The dog panted, eating up the attention.

Annie leaned against the doorjamb and sipped her beverage as to not interrupt the scene playing out in front of her. After listening to Daniel last night and understanding his fears and regrets, her heart swelled. The man was trying with Lily.

"You know, Shadow, I was scared yesterday when I couldn't find Annie in her office."

The dog leaned forward and licked Daniel's cheek.

"Thanks, buddy. I needed that." He wiped the dog slobber off his face and glanced at Lily. The antics of the pair had a slight twitch of a smile flash on the girl's lips. As if satisfied with the results, Daniel continued. "Then Izzie and I worked together, and we found her. It's really nice to know I can count on my sister. She'll help me no matter what happens." He blinked as if realizing what he had said, then ran a hand down Shadow's head and back. "You know, boy, you're a good listener. Don't ya think, Lily?"

Her daughter's eyes shot to Daniel, then the dog, and back. She stared at the man sprawled out on the floor. Her little forehead scrunched. Annie wished she could be privy to the thoughts that swirled in her daughter's mind.

To Annie's shock, Lily nodded and returned to playing.

Daniel's eyes widened. He patted Shadow one more time. "Lily, your momma and I are heading into work. Miss Hannah and Mr. Logan, along with Shadow here, will be at the ranch with you. If you need anything, let them know. We're only a phone call away."

Lily continued to play with the stuffed animals, but Annie could tell she'd heard every word Daniel had said.

"Hey, you two." She pushed off the wall and strode in. "It's time for Daniel and me to go to the rodeo grounds for a little while. We'll be back soon. You and Shadow have fun today." Annie kissed Lily on the side of her head. A ball of emotion lodged in her throat when her daughter leaned into her. Her baby was still in there somewhere. "Come on, Daniel. My office won't organize itself." Trying to stay lighthearted wasn't easy. She just wanted to curl up next to Lily and pretend bad things didn't exist.

"On it." He stood. "Shadow, my man, you're the dog in charge. I have to go. If you want to talk some more, you'll have to do it with Lily." He patted the furball. "Have a good day, Shadow. You too, Lily." Daniel followed Annie out of the room.

Once in the kitchen, she turned to him. "Thank you."

He tilted his head. Confusion flickered across his face. "For what?"

"For showing Lily she could talk to Shadow. For being the man I knew you'd grow up to be. For trying with my daughter, even though I know it's hard for you. For basically, everything." What more could she say?

Daniel's hands cupped her cheek. "You never have to thank me for doing what's right." His eyes searched hers, looking for permission to kiss her.

She nodded.

He dipped his head and inched closer. "Are you sure?"

"I'm sure."

A throat cleared behind them.

Daniel straightened and took two steps back.

"Sorry to interrupt." Logan's gaze dropped to the floor. He scratched the back of his neck. "Thought you might want to know that Izzie plans to meet you at Annie's office to go over a few things we've discovered."

"Thanks, Logan. We were heading out in a couple of minutes." Daniel's hand skimmed down her arm and squeezed her fingers before he let go.

"No problem. And again, sorry to interrupt."

Why did Annie feel like a kid caught with her hand in the cookie jar? For the love of everything, she was a grown woman and shouldn't care what Logan thought. She chuckled.

"What's so funny?"

"We're grown adults, and I feel like I'm five."

Daniel smirked. "Same here. What do ya say we get out of here?"

"Sounds like a great idea. I hate leaving Lily, but I can't

abandon my work either. Plus, it gives us the opportunity to poke around and figure out who's behind all the attacks."

"I realize I won't be able to stay by your side all day, but after yesterday, I don't want you walking around by yourself."

"Normally, I'd complain you're stepping on my independence, but I'm not too fond of the idea of wandering the rodeo grounds alone."

"I'm glad we agree." Daniel gave her a lopsided grin.

His kindness, his concern, his dedication to her safety released a hundred butterflies loose in her belly. She'd walked away once—not by choice. This time? The choice was his. And she prayed he wanted her and Lily in his life.

They moved to his truck and got in. Daniel drove down the lane, kicking up dirt and gravel as he went.

Annie watched the trees and open pastures zip by. "I wonder what Izzie found out."

"I'd like to know that as well. I'm surprised she hasn't called me. I mean, I am her brother and one of her deputies. But nooooo, she talked to Logan. How dare she call her husband and not me." His fake exasperation made her want to laugh.

"I agree. That's the weirdest thing." Annie rolled her eyes. "You haven't changed, have you?"

He lifted her hand and kissed the back of it. "Nope. And I don't plan to either."

"But you *will* stop hiding behind the humor, right?"

A big sigh filled the cab. "I'll work on it."

"That's all I ask." The man had suffered enough. Annie wanted to help him heal.

A while later they pulled into the rodeo grounds parking lot and came to a stop near her new office. Izzie leaned against the wall, studying her phone.

"Appears as though sis isn't going to make us wait." Daniel dropped from the truck and waited by the front bumper for her to join him.

"She looks tired."

Daniel's eyes narrowed. "You're right. More so than normal."

Izzie pushed off the building. "Good morning, you two."

"Hi, Izzie. We heard you had information." Annie unlocked her office for the day and gestured for the two siblings to go inside.

Once the door shut, Izzie scanned the interior. "I do." She closed her eyes for a moment then stared straight at Annie and Daniel. "A teen died from a fentanyl overdose late last night. I have the lab running a chemical comparison. But what you don't know is that when we collected Deputy Bonner's clothes for the investigation, he had a sample tucked in his pocket. I'm assuming it was evidence. I got the results back this morning." Izzie's gaze locked on to Annie. "It's hospital grade. We checked Rollins General, and nothing is amiss. I admit, it's a stretch, but the only link to a hospital is the threat against you. And with what you told us about your departure from San Antonio, we have to consider a connection."

Annie sucked in a breath. Her mind spun at the implication. "Layton Pope? How? He's in San Antonio—hours away. Dr. Gregory promised to keep me informed of Layton's whereabouts, but I'm sure he's dealing with family matters after Karly's death. So, I'm not sure if Dr. Pope left the city."

Daniel lifted his cowboy hat and scratched his head. "Maybe he has. Maybe he hasn't. But it's possible the drugs have."

"You mean Dr. Pope wasn't just stealing for his own benefit?" If what they proposed was true, how would she ever keep Lily safe and have a normal life? Whatever that was. She'd never experienced normal.

"According to what you've told us, Pope's using, but he could also be a distributor." Daniel shrugged. "Remember the car by the loading dock?"

"You think that was a drug deal?" Annie shook her head. "He can't take that much without flags popping up long before I reported him."

"Pope's worked in San Antonio's medical system for years. He probably knows a dozen ways around a pharmacy inventory log. He's not stealing it by the duffel bag full. Consider this. What if he's manipulating the system—padding supply orders, logging doses that were never administered, and dumping extras through fake patient files. It's a pure guess, but it's possible."

"Izzie, you have a devious mind." Annie rubbed her forehead. Bile burned the back of her throat. "He knows how to bypass every checkpoint. He could control the system."

"The theory is solid, except for one point." Daniel sighed. "If we're correct, this is bigger than Pope and some random dealer in Rollins."

"For a widespread network, there's no way Pope could supply enough drugs."

"He could if he's one of several doctors involved throughout the state." Izzie's words punched Annie in the gut. "And is linked to someone associated with the rodeos, fairs, or carnival, giving them access to more young people." Izzie pinched the bridge of her nose. "Poisoning our teens has to stop. Too many are dying because of it. I'll contact the DEA and run this by them, then I'm calling Logan to see if he can dig something up on that angle."

"I feel like we're trying to read tracks in a dust storm." Daniel extracted a key from his pocket and held it up. "We need to find Bonner's evidence. That might put us on the right path and stop our speculating."

The key in Daniel's hand. The one Deputy Bonner had trusted her with. That small piece of metal tormented her. She hadn't kept her promise to the dying officer. "Give me about twenty minutes to get this place rodeo ready, then we can search for what that key goes to."

"Izzie?" Daniel deferred to his sister.

"We need that evidence." Izzie flicked her hand toward the key. "You two see if you can figure out Bonner's secret hiding spot, and I'll continue to investigate the overdose deaths and place those phone calls. Hopefully, our findings will meet in the middle, and we can put those responsible behind bars."

Plans in place, Izzie excused herself, and Annie and Daniel got busy. Fifteen minutes later, earlier than expected, they studied the shape of the key.

Daniel flipped it over in his palm. "A footlocker maybe?"

"Or a lockbox or tool chest. There are too many options." Annie checked her phone for the time. "We have four hours before we have to prep for the rodeo."

Daniel tucked the key into his pocket, out of sight. "Let's start at the carnival since Bonner worked there undercover."

They stepped outside, and Annie secured her office door. "That'll be like finding a specific grain of sand on a mile-long stretch of beach."

"You're right. The possibilities seem endless, but we have to start somewhere."

"Then lead the way." Annie rubbed her arms, chasing away the shiver of fear threatening to strangle her.

As they moved through the crowds, someone bumped her shoulder, throwing her off balance. She bit her lip to keep a scream from escaping and stutter-stepped to keep from falling. Her previous attack at the carnival had her jumping at the press of people.

I get it, Lily. I really do. She had a new appreciation for her daughter's trauma response.

The hair on the back of her neck prickled. She lifted her shoulders to fend off the shiver snaking up her back and scanned the busy area, searching for the cause.

Was her attacker here? Did he have eyes on her? Or was her imagination running wild?

Daniel wrapped his arm around Annie's waist to steady her. The woman was jumpier than a long-tailed cat in a room full of rocking chairs. He tightened his hold and wove through the crowd. The calliope music mixed with the thump of bean bags hitting the board and the pop, pop, pop of darts thrown at balloons. His nerves strung tight, ready to snap. But it was the sickening sweet warm sugar mingling with the diesel engines from the rides that nauseated him.

He pointed to the edge of one of the trailers that held the baseball throw. "Let's go to the back lot."

Annie's strained nod concerned him.

Steering them around the game, he stepped over the power cords snaking across the ground and tugged her into the makeshift alley between the trailers and campers that housed the carnival employees.

The chaotic sounds dimmed. Daniel puffed out a breath. His ears thanked him for leaving the racket behind. He shifted to face Annie.

Her gaze darted from one shadowy area to another.

"I've got you, Annie."

She closed her eyes. "I know, but it doesn't change the grip fear has on me."

"You have every right to be scared. I'm not letting my attention waver this time."

A smile curved her lips. "And that makes being out here more manageable."

He tucked a stray wisp of hair behind her ear. "Let's get started."

"Lead the way."

The trust she put in him made him feel invincible. But his inner voice reminded him to stay alert.

Daniel strode to a string of lockers in clear view under the game trailers. He retrieved the key. "Watch for anyone coming into the area. I don't want to announce what we're doing."

She spun with her back to him on lookout duty while he moved from one box to the next, trying the key.

"Nothing." He stood and gestured to a metal box with two compartments a couple of campers over.

"Do you really think we'll find anything here?" The defeat in Annie's tone worried him.

"I'm not sure we'll find it today, but I have every confidence that we'll discover the evidence Bonner hid at some point and close this case for him."

Her shoulders drooped. "You're right."

Daniel plastered on a grin. What was the saying? Fake it till you make it? "Can you please say that again so I can record it?"

Annie chuckled and smacked his arm. "Stop that."

"What?" He held his palms up and shrugged.

"You're a dork." The *woe is me* cloak lifted from Annie, and she smiled. Big. Beautiful. Carefree. If only for a moment.

Daniel would make a hundred jokes a day to see Annie happy.

A shiver like icy fingers crawled up his spine and whispered across the back of his neck. Someone was watching them. He spun. A shadow moved beyond the last trailer, tucking out of sight.

"What is it? Is someone out there?" Annie's gaze frantically darted from one trailer to the next.

"We need to finish our search and get out of here."

"Daniel?"

He exhaled. "Fine. I'm not sure. But I'm not willing to stick around any longer than we have to and find out."

"Where to next?" She gripped his hand a bit tighter than normal.

"We need to put ourselves in Bonner's mind." Normally

he'd close his eyes and allow his imagination to take over. Today, no way. He stared at a faraway spot. "If I were Bonner, undercover as a carnie, and I had collected evidence that I hid until I could pass it on to my handler, where would I put it?"

"Not in my camper. That's the first place someone would look," Annie suggested.

"Good. Keep going."

"I'd want it close. That way I could keep an eye on it."

"I agree. Within visual distance." Daniel focused on the camper Bonner had lived in. The deputies had examined it after the man's death and found nothing of importance. "That's Bonner's temporary home over there."

Annie tugged him along as she strode toward the structure and stood in front of a small window. "I'm assuming this is the bedroom."

"That would be my guess."

She placed her back against the aluminum siding under the window.

"What are you doing?"

"What you said to do? Pretending I'm Bonner." She waved her hand in an arc. "I would want to be able to see my hiding spot from my bedroom."

"Okay. I'll bite. Why?"

"As an undercover carnie, the only time I'd come to my camper would be for sleep and maybe a quick meal. So, it would make sense that he'd want to be able to roll over and peek out the curtain to check on his evidence."

Daniel's jaw dropped. "You're brilliant."

"No. I'm used to thinking outside the box as an emergency medical physician. Certain traumas require a bit of an investigator's perspective. Knowing how injuries happen can help us make better treatment plans."

"Want a job as a detective? If so, you're hired."

"No, thank you. I'll stick with medicine." She nudged him with her shoulder.

The lighthearted banter soothed over the missing years. Could he have a future with this woman? Daniel stiffened and jerked his attention to the end of the makeshift alley. The same sensation as earlier crept across him.

"What is it?" Annie went from relaxed to on high alert.

"I'm not sure. Just a feeling." He was sure of one thing. Someone slinked along the edge of the trailers. Watching. Waiting. "Let's find the evidence and get out of here." His spidey senses weren't just tingling. They had sparked into a full-fledged fire alert freak-out.

"You're scaring me."

"I'm sorry, but I want you away from here."

"Fine." Annie straightened and placed her back against the camper once again.

He mimicked her stance and studied each box, every dark crevice where the evidence might be stashed. A place or item that would require a key to open.

"What about that?" Daniel pointed to a rust-streaked electrical panel next to a container holding supply trunks labeled Costumes, Utility Bin, Cleaning Supplies, and such.

"The electrical panel?"

"No. The trunks. Think about it. Hide the evidence in plain sight."

Annie glanced at the camper window and drew a line with her eyes to the trunks. "You might be on to something."

"From your lips to God's ears."

She chuckled. "Oh, I'm praying all right."

"Come on." He strode over, checked to make sure no one had joined them in the alley, and opened the first trunk, labeled Costumes, and flipped the lid open. Daniel opened the trunk and rifled through the clothes. "Nope. Not this one."

"What about a false bottom?"

He raised a brow at her. “You watch too much TV.”

“I do not.” She rolled her eyes.

Grasping at any possibility, Daniel examined the box and tapped on the bottom panel. “Nice try, but there’s nothing there.”

He checked the one labeled Utility Bin then the cleaning supply one with the same results. “The last one’s the charm?” He crouched in front of the first aid supply trunk.

“I think you have the saying wrong, but in this situation, I certainly hope so.” Annie leaned over him, hand clasped against her chest.

He doubted Bonner hid the evidence in one of these boxes, but he had to try. He dug through the medical supplies.

“It’s not here.” The defeat in Annie’s tone was unmistakable.

His shoulders drooped. “We’ll keep looking. It has to be here somewhere.” He lowered the lid. He tilted his head and squinted at the electrical box. It had a small door that looked out of place. “Hold on.” Daniel pushed aside the containers and opened it. A lockbox sat inside.

Annie knelt and grabbed his arm. “Do you think?”

His pulse raced. He closed his eyes and threw up a prayer. After scanning the area one more time, he removed the box.

“Oh, please, Lord, let it be what we’re looking for.”

“Amen to that.” Daniel eased the key into the lock and turned it. The latch clicked. He lifted the lid. “There’s a large flat envelope.”

Her grip on his arm tightened.

He retrieved the package, sliding it from its hiding spot. Not willing to linger, he stood and threaded his fingers with Annie’s. “Your office. Now.”

She nodded and, without argument, followed his lead.

The air shifted. Suffocating. Unnatural. Wrong. The sensation scraped over his nerves.

A gunshot rang out.

* * *

Arms wrapped around Annie and she slammed against the ground. A bullet thudded into the dirt next to her. Pebbles peppered her skin. Daniel rolled her under the game trailer, his body shielding her from the gunman.

Another shot cracked, hitting the metal above them.

"Stay down." Daniel shifted and drew his weapon.

Annie pressed flat to the gravel. The cheerful carnival music clashed with the gunfire echoing through the alley behind the games and rides.

Heavy footsteps pounded closer.

She caught a flash of movement through the strip of light from under the trailer.

Daniel held up a hand.

Her lungs burned with the effort to keep still. She prayed the shooter couldn't hear her heartbeat thundering against her rib cage.

The footsteps slowed. Stopped. Right outside. Boots turned in a slow circle.

Annie's stomach twisted. Her first instinct screamed to crawl deeper, but Daniel's palm rested on her shoulder. She peered at him. He shook his head. Swallowing down her instinct to run, she inhaled and counted to ten.

The man shifted, and the silence stretched tight as a wire.

Daniel's hand squeezed once. He mouthed, *Run*.

He rolled from under the trailer, aiming his weapon. "Police!"

The mystery man pulled the trigger, but the shot went wide. The shooter ducked behind another trailer.

When Daniel fired, Annie scrambled out the far side, the gravel piercing her knees. She pushed to her feet and bolted into the maze of campers. Shouts erupted. A bullet pinged on the corner of a trailer near her head. She ducked lower and ran harder to escape the maze of trailers.

"Annie!" Daniel's voice rang behind her.

She zigzagged between stacked crates and coiled power cords. Her lungs burned. Another shot whizzed past. She skidded around a trailer. Dead end. In her haste, she'd gotten turned around. A jumble of broken-down crates and tangled cords blocked the way.

The shooter rounded the corner, gun raised. A ski mask hid his features.

Her breath caught.

Daniel slammed into him from the side. Both men crashed into the crates. Wood splintered and cords scattered across the dirt.

The man recovered and rammed Daniel into the trailer wall with a thud. Daniel shoved back, his jaw clenched. He raised his weapon. "Don't move!"

The gunman froze, eyes darting between her and Daniel. Then, with a grunt, he kicked a stack of storage containers. Tools and miscellaneous parts clattered toward her. She lost her balance and stumbled into Daniel.

Boots thundered behind her.

"Drop it!" Izzie's voice cut sharp and commanding.

The shooter cursed and spun, firing. Sparks burst from a metal drum as the bullet ricocheted.

Another set of boots pounded in. Deputy Lane dove beside Izzie, gun raised. "Sheriff, I've got him covered!"

Izzie hunched and circled to the right.

Annie lay on the dirt and shielded her head.

Daniel went left, but the shooter tore into the shadows.

Izzie and Lane gave chase.

Daniel helped Annie off the ground. His chest heaved from the adrenaline. "You okay?"

Unable to trust her voice, she nodded.

A few minutes later, Izzie strode forward with Lane flanking her. "We lost him. Is anyone hurt?"

"Just rattled." Annie glanced at her palms and knees. "Maybe a few Band-Aids required, but other than that, I'm good."

Daniel clenched his teeth. He locked his gaze where the gunman vanished. He tugged her close and kissed the top of her head. "I'm so sorry."

Annie choked back a sob. If she never laid eyes on another carnival it would be too soon.

The room closed in on Daniel. He'd rushed Annie to her medical office, away from the chaos and threat. Now, he paced from one end to the other of the small reception area, waiting for his sheriff sister to finish giving orders at the carnival. Running a hand through his hair, his gaze fixed on the small stack of photographs that lay on Annie's desk. Finding the evidence should have answered questions, not created more. He glanced at his watch. The rodeo time crept up on him. Soon he and Annie would have to leave for their other duties. Izzie had better get here soon.

"I don't understand these images." Annie's eyes held a lingering shadow from the events over the past couple of days as she studied the photos.

"Rodeo vendors. A couple of the carnies." Daniel fanned the pictures. He didn't have time to thoroughly examine each one. The details blurred into a montage of faces, trailers, and storage containers. "Bonner must have figured it out before he died. But I don't have a clue to what."

"I can't imagine going undercover like that. He stumbled onto something that got him killed." She rubbed her arms. "The poor man didn't have backup."

Daniel nodded, a muscle ticking in his jaw. "Where is Izzie? We need to go. The rodeo starts soon."

The door swung open.

Daniel drew his weapon, grabbed Annie, and jerked her behind him.

Izzie strode in and took in the scene. “Whoa. Sorry, bro. Didn’t mean to startle you.”

Daniel clutched his chest and re-holstered his gun. “Don’t do that.”

“A bit edgy, aren’t we?”

“You could say that after the guy shot at Annie not more than thirty minutes ago.”

“Understandable.” Izzie stepped next to the desk. “What do you have?”

He pointed to the photos. “It’s not the smoking gun we’d hoped for. It’s just faces and pictures of general scenes. Rodeo vendors. Carnival workers. Trailers. Groups of people. I wish Bonner were here to tell us what we’re looking at.”

“Wouldn’t that be nice.” Izzie flipped through the images. “Carnival crews and vendors make sense. They stay longer, they have trailers, storage—even supply deliveries. They blend in.” Izzie gathered the stack and slid them into the envelope.

“Someone who knows how to hide in plain sight.” Annie sunk onto the leather couch. Fatigue laced her features.

“Exactly.” Izzie looked at Daniel. “I’ll run them through the system and see if I can identify any of these people. Since you’ll both be working tonight, I’ll make sure a couple of deputies patrol the rodeo grounds in addition to the normal security and keep an eye on things.”

Annie glanced at the clock. “We need to head out.”

“Get going.” Izzie waved them toward the door. “I’ll secure the office and dig into this information. I’ll let you know what I find.”

“Talk to ya later, sis.” Daniel held the door open, and Annie exited. He wrapped his arm around her waist and led her to the arena.

Rodeo participants jogged through the barn, kicking up dust and hay.

Daniel scanned the busy area.

The medical office had felt like a cage, but the crowded and chaotic rodeo grounds had jolted his nerves. He had a sinking feeling they'd stepped into the crosshairs of the killer.

NINE

"Lily's with Logan. Izzie will join them when she calls it quits for the day. I'm sorry I couldn't stay with her."

Annie gripped her cell phone against her ear as she listened to Miss Hannah's apology, wishing not for the first time that she and Daniel didn't have the rodeo tonight. She rested her arms on the fence and toed the dirt next to the chutes on the edge of the arena. Hannah had taken her daughter to Logan and Izzie's farm not far from Stone Creek Ranch. Lily was safe. Especially with a navy SEAL watching out for her. Annie had a job to do, and Miss Hannah had committed to staying with her granddaughter, Lexi, while Daniel's brother, Cooper, and his wife, Grace, went to an overnight conference together.

"It's fine. I know we aren't your only priority. I appreciate everything you've done for us." Annie closed her eyes. She couldn't complain. Hannah had gone above and beyond to help her and Lily. It was just that Stone Creek Ranch had security measures.

"I still feel bad uprooting Lily, even if it's just for the evening until you and Daniel are free. But Logan had work that he had to do from his secure network at home."

No matter the time, she and Daniel had decided to pick Lily up after the rodeo and take her back to the ranch. Annie hadn't wanted her daughter to sleep all night in another strange place.

"I understand. You've been very generous. Lily will be fine for the evening. She seems okay, if you take away the fact she won't talk and the nightmares."

"You and Daniel think she saw something, don't you?"

Miss Hannah's question bounced around in her brain. "Yeah, I think Lily knows more than we're aware of. I'm guessing she saw someone or something when Karly was killed. She said a few things to Shadow. It's a start, but until she opens up, we'll never know. I wish—"

Annie spun at the scuffing sound behind her. Her breath quickened as she scanned the area, but no one was there.

"Annie? Is everything okay?"

She settled her heart rate. "I thought I heard something, but I guess it was my imagination." Or not. "I better go. The rodeo is starting in a little bit. We'll pick Lily up later tonight, probably around eleven thirty or so, and take her back to the ranch."

"I'll let Logan and Izzie know."

"Thanks." She hung up and examined her surroundings. The events from the past couple of days had made her jumpy. But who could blame her? Annie tucked the phone in her pocket and strode to the section of the arena where she'd watch the rodeo, praying that her medical expertise wasn't needed.

"Hey, there." Decked out in his bullfighting attire, Daniel joined her in the designated fenced-off area that allowed her easy access to the arena.

"Hi." She smiled. The man made her feel like a teenager again.

"Are you ready for tonight?"

"I should be the one asking you that." She perused his outfit. "Still playing with bulls, I see." Annie loved the fun easy conversations. There hadn't been enough of those since she returned to Rollins. Or for the years after her best friend, Libby, had died. Even with the threat against her, she'd enjoy this brief moment of levity.

"They're just like toddlers with an attitude, only bigger."

"Much bigger." She reached for his hand and squeezed his fingers. "Please be careful."

"Always am."

She searched his eyes, looking for the truth. And there it was. Full of confidence. Ready to protect those in harm's way.

"I mean, with you there to pick up my pieces, it's even better." He waggled his eyebrows.

Annie whacked him in the stomach. "Stop that."

Daniel threw his head back and laughed. The deep belly laugh she'd missed. "I'm kidding. This is what I do. My partner, Ronnie, and I are good. Maybe not as in sync as Grace and I were, but we can read each other pretty well."

Back in the day, Grace and Daniel had an unreal connection in the arena, making them the best bullfighting duo known around the circuit. Which worked out great since they protected Daniel's brother, Cooper, during his bull riding days. Annie had no idea how Grace watched the man she'd secretly loved risk his life every rodeo. Of course, that's what Annie had done. But instead of being on the back of a bull, Daniel faced off with them.

"Just don't do anything stupid and get hurt."

"Don't plan to." He lifted her hand and kissed her knuckles. "Let's get you comfortable. I need to go chat with the riders before the events start."

She settled in her special seat near the gate. He handed her a water bottle from the cooler Keats supplied. "Thanks. Stay safe."

He tipped his cowboy hat. "Always, ma'am."

Annie rolled her eyes. "Get." She shooed him away and inhaled. Home. That's what the rodeo and Rollins felt like. Never in her wildest dreams did she imagine coming back here and reconnecting with Daniel. But here she was. Now if Izzie and

Daniel could arrest whoever had murdered Bonner and Karly, tried to abduct Lily, and tried to kill her, life would be good.

The evening had progressed with only minor injuries. A few rope burns, a finger dislocation, and a bruised foot from getting stepped on by a horse. Nothing serious. The last event—bull riding—had Annie's nerves on edge. She had no idea why. She'd witnessed the two-thousand-pound animals do their thing before, but for some reason, tonight was different. The evidence she and Daniel had uncovered weighed heavily on her. The information Bonner left hinted at either a carnie or rodeo participant smuggling drugs inside the community. But that was strictly an assumption based on what they'd seen on the photos in the envelope.

Three riders in, Annie scanned the crowd. Was her attacker and gunman out there—watching—waiting for another opportunity to kill her?

Gah! She had to stop with the *what ifs*. She had a job to do.

The bull bucked the next rider off, and the cowboy hit the dirt with a thud. She grimaced at the power behind the landing. On instinct, she stood and gathered her bag. Daniel and Ronnie skillfully handled the bull.

With the arena clear, Annie rushed to the cowboy lying on the ground approximately twenty feet or so in front of the chute. She assessed his injuries and called for the paramedics to take the poor guy to the hospital. It appeared he'd broken a couple of ribs and had a concussion on top of that.

A little while later the medics pushed the gurney through the gate. She knelt and gathered her things.

"Annie!" Daniel's frantic tone sent shivers up her spine.

She shot to her feet and spun. A bull with the features of a Brahman bloodline came charging toward her. Her head screamed to run, but her feet froze in place.

Arms wrapped her waist and flung her to the side. She

hit the ground with an oof. A body cocooned her from the fierce animal.

"Ronnie!"

"On it!"

The words flitted on the air just out of reach. Her brain scrambled to form a picture of what had transpired.

The weight lifted, and her lungs filled with precious oxygen. She blinked. Vivid green eyes stared back at her.

"Are you okay?" Daniel brushed the hair from her face.

"I think so. What happened?" She accepted his hand and sat upright, getting her bearings.

"A bull got loose and aimed right for you."

"No one else got hurt?" Her pulse raced at the idea of an innocent person injured.

Daniel helped her to stand then walked her to the exit. "The bull slammed the chute open and into one of the gate men, but he's up and walking. I'm sure he'll have bruises tomorrow."

"Do you think it was on purpose?" She wobbled on unsteady legs. Facing a huge animal like that did funny things to a person's composure.

Daniel jerked to a stop. "I hadn't until you said that."

"Everything seemed to work for the first half of the competition. Why now? The only difference is me going out there to help."

Daniel raked his experienced law enforcement gaze around the arena. "I want you out of here."

"I can't leave, and you know it. We still have bull riders left to compete."

He puffed out a breath. "That may be true, but I still don't like it."

Annie brushed the dirt from her jeans and T-shirt she'd chosen to wear for her first official night on the job. So much for wearing that shirt again. The memories of almost getting stomped by a bull would always be tied to it. Ridiculous—

yes—but it was what it was. Inhaling, she refocused on Daniel, refusing to unravel, no matter how justified it might be. "Go. Do your thing. I'll be on alert for anything out of the ordinary while you finish up."

A loud whistle broke their conversation. Ronnie motioned for Daniel to join him.

Daniel glanced at his partner then returned his focus to Annie. "If you're sure."

"I'm okay. I promise."

He studied her for a moment then nodded and headed out to join Ronnie for the next ride.

Annie's nerves danced like live wires. The more she thought about what happened, the more she was convinced the gate latch not working hadn't been an accident. Now she just wanted to hold her baby in her arms for her own comfort and to convince herself that Lily was safe.

On Daniel's way back into the arena, he caught the eye of security and gestured to one of the men to stand guard next to Annie. He worried that whoever had let the bull loose would come back and try again. He had a job to do, and it worried him that his divided attention would give her attacker another opening.

Annie wrapped her arms around her middle and gave the guard a forced smile.

Her reaction sent daggers through his heart. The woman was shaken worse than she'd let on.

After the final ride and closing remarks by the emcee and with security near Annie, Daniel chatted with the men at the chutes. They all agreed that the chute had worked—until it hadn't. Obviously tampered with. But how hadn't anyone seen or heard anything? When that Brahman charged Annie, his heart had stopped. Only by the grace of God had he and Ronnie saved her from becoming rodeo roadkill.

Between rides, he'd sneaked peeks at her. Even from a distance, he'd caught the way she searched the crowd. The way her hand brushed against the bruises on her neck. His stomach tightened. Annie was tough, but no one walked away from the recent close calls without internal scars.

Releasing a lung full of air through pursed lips, he bid the guys goodbye and strode to the special area Keats had designated for Annie.

"Thanks, man. Could you hang around until we leave?" Daniel shook the security guard's hand.

"Whatever you need." The man jerked his head toward the barn entrance. "I'll be over there."

"Appreciate it." He turned his attention to Annie and hitched his cleat onto the rail fence. "Ready to go?"

Her faraway gaze latched on to him, and she blinked. "Once I put my bag in my office and secure the tablet with the documents I filled out from the injuries, I'll be more than ready to head out."

"Sounds like a plan." He pulled his shirt away from his chest. Between the sweat and the dirt, the material clung to his skin. His long shorts weren't much better after yanking Annie out of the way of the bull and diving on top of her to protect her. "And I'd love to change out of this getup."

"Why don't you clean up in my office bathroom while I take care of these things." She held up a small duffel and clipboard as she moved into the connecting barn. "It has a small shower you can use if you'd like."

"That would be amazing. I could kiss you for that idea." His brain froze. Had he really just said that?

Annie stumbled and spun to face him. Her eyes wide.

"I mean…it was just…" He blew out a long breath. Wow. He'd dug himself a hole with that one. "I'm not saying I hate that idea, because I don't. But it's not what I meant." Daniel dipped his chin. The woman had tilted his world with her abrupt appearance in Rollins, and he still felt off balance. He'd crushed on her for years and then she'd disappeared. Not that her absence took away his attraction to her. Who wouldn't want the delightful girl he'd known? She personified empathy and kindness. And knowing what he now knew about her mother, he wondered how Annie had maintained her sweet nature. He wanted to kiss her. Had almost kissed her at the ranch house, but Logan had interrupted. Something he'd give his brother-in-law grief about later.

"I can't say kissing you sounds horrible either, but I understand what you meant. Let's take care of business so we can go get Lily."

Okay, then. A smile tugged on his lips. *Later, Annie. Once the crazy settles, we'll explore that kiss.*

At the medical office, she put her supplies away and stored her tablet while Daniel cleaned up.

He opened the bathroom door, and steam wafted into the front room. Hair wet, Daniel combed it with his fingers and slung his bag over his shoulder. "Ready when you are."

"I'm done. Let me lock up on the way out." The keys jiggled in her trembling hands. It took her several tries before she succeeded in locking the door.

Outside, the chaos from the rodeo had vanished. Even the sheep had quit bleating. Only the lights and music from the carnival hung in the night air. Annie flinched at the shrill calliope music and clutched her duffel tighter.

Daniel hurried her to his truck and dismissed the guard. He wanted her away from the park—now.

She eased into his vehicle.

He examined the surroundings while he circled the front of his truck, looking for anything that spelled trouble.

Without words, they left the rodeo grounds and drove past the carnival on their way out of the park. The occasional streetlamp dotted the road until they hit the county highway. The outline of trees stretched along the shoulder. Daniel watched the rearview mirror for unexpected company, but nothing appeared out of the norm. But after Annie got run off the road, he wouldn't let his guard down.

He peeked over at Annie. She sat, staring out the window into the dark. Her reflection showed a woman deep in thought. He tried to sort through the memories and make sense of the past. Annie had loved the town and community, even if she'd been the girl from the wrong side of the tracks. Her words, not his. So, why hadn't her mom stayed in Rollins?

Give it up, man. According to Annie, that's not an answer you'll ever get. Don't waste time on the hurts of the past.

He turned down the long dirt road to Logan and Izzie's place. "Almost there. Logan bought the old place for Izzie. My sister has always loved this farm. Not big enough to actually have cattle or crops. Just enough for her to ride her horse. Logan even has feelers out to purchase a few goats. And don't tell Izzie, but he's also looking at a couple of llamas." His sister and those odd-looking animals. He shook his head. And people called *him* ridiculous.

Annie jerked her gaze to him. "Llamas? Why?"

"Because he loves Izzie and wants to give her everything. And that woman loves those crazy animals for whatever reason."

She chuckled. "Makes perfect sense."

"As if." Not so much. "But yeah, Logan's good for my sister, and she's good for him. Just don't tell them I said that. I have to maintain my brother status that no one is worthy of her."

Annie chuckled. The light sound lifted a layer of worry from his shoulders.

Daniel put the truck into Park. "I'm guessing Lily's asleep by now. Knowing my sister, she'd tucked her into bed in one of the extra bedrooms. It'll give us the opportunity to chat with them for a moment before we head back to the ranch. I'd like to hear what they've discovered."

"I'm in. However, let's not stay long." The truck's interior light spotlighted the weariness etched on her face.

"We won't. Just long enough to get an update." He met her in front of the truck and laced their fingers together. They walked to the front door, both exhausted from the day.

Daniel knocked.

The door opened. A tired Logan greeted them. "Hey, guys. Come on in and have a seat. And before you ask, Lily's fine. She's asleep in the downstairs bedroom."

"Thank you. I didn't like leaving her but knowing you had her covered made things easier."

"Anytime. She's a good kid."

Daniel tensed out of habit. He was a work in progress when it came to children, but he agreed with his brother-in-law. Putting his insecurities aside, he led Annie into the living room.

Izzie lounged on the couch under a pile of documents with Shadow lying on the floor under her feet. "Yo, bro. Annie. How'd tonight go?"

Daniel collapsed onto the love seat and tugged Annie next to him. "It was exhilarating, if you consider Annie almost getting trampled exciting."

"Say what now?" Izzie sat up straight and tossed the file onto the coffee table. Shadow lifted his head, studying her, then laid his snout on his paws and closed his eyes.

"A bull rider got thrown, and she came out to assess his injuries. Another bull in one of the chutes got loose and came at her."

"Well, obviously everything is okay, but what happened?" Izzie sat, legs crisscrossed, holding her ankles.

"Daniel tackled me and protected me from getting stomped on."

Izzie drilled him with a stare. No words needed. He understood her demand without closed captions.

Casual tone on purpose, Daniel straightened his legs and crossed his ankles. His insides were anything but relaxed. "Ronnie took care of the bull while I focused on Annie. It all worked out, and everyone is safe. I talked with the guys after the rodeo ended. No one had answers to the critter getting loose. And Neil is sporting the bruises from the gate slamming into him."

Logan scratched the stubble on his jaw. "Our killer has access to the rodeo grounds. As in undetected if he pulled that off."

"It would seem like it." Daniel's stomach churned as he remembered the chute opening and the bull lowering its head, aiming straight for Annie.

Izzie gestured to the file she'd tossed aside. "I contacted Dr. Gregory like you suggested, Annie. He's grieving his niece's death but is concerned about you. Earlier tonight, I received additional information from him. Dr. Pope has not left San Antonio, so he's not the person directly responsible for your attacks." Izzie held up her hand, stopping Daniel from arguing her point. "That doesn't mean he didn't hire someone to do his dirty work. However, with Logan's help, the evidence you were able to retrieve from Bonner's hiding spot, and the department's connections with the DEA, we discovered that Marshall County and the surrounding counties are part of a fentanyl drug pipeline."

"What?" Daniel expected a drug dealer targeting the area for new blood, so to speak. But a pipeline? "That screams a large organization and not a contained business."

"Exactly." Izzie collapsed against the cushions. "With the other sheriffs' blessings, I've pulled every drug overdose in the region. Because ODs happen at various times with no pattern, we hadn't considered a connection. Now that we are looking, we've found a link to the increase in drugs and deaths. It follows the rodeos and by extension the carnival."

"How did we miss that?" Daniel closed his eyes and exhaled. "What else?"

"We don't have much, but with that knowledge and Bonner's pictures, we can narrow things down to a carnie or a vendor. Although I have no idea how it ties to Karly's death."

"What about the rodeo participants?" Annie asked.

"It's possible, but think about it." Her legs unfolded and her feet hit the floor, avoiding Shadow. She leaned forward, elbows on her knees. "These are competitors. They show up with their horses, maybe a camper, and a few personal bags. No supply chains. No storage setups. There's no practical way for them to move product unnoticed—not in quantity anyway."

"And the rodeo community watch each other like hawks, especially after the craziness that happened over the last year. Word would've gotten out." Daniel hadn't let his guard down after his sister had come close to getting herself killed saving Logan's twin, Lisa.

"Exactly." Izzie nodded. "The carnival crew and vendors? They're different. They stay longer, they have trailers, storage—even supply deliveries. They blend in."

Annie's gaze scanned the small group. "So, we're not looking at a rider. We're looking at someone embedded. Someone who knows how to hide in plain sight."

"With your close call tonight, I'd say it's someone attached to the rodeo. A carnie couldn't move unnoticed and tamper with the chute gate." Daniel searched his brain for who it might be.

A low growl rumbled from Shadow. The dog launched from his place on the floor and raced down the hall. Deep frightening barks filled the air.

"Lily!" Logan shot to his feet and tore after his dog.

Annie gasped and chased after Logan.

He and Izzie hit the bedroom entrance as Logan flung it open. Shadow dashed to the window, his barks becoming more intense.

Lily tucked herself into a ball on the bed. A whimper escaped as her little eyes focused on the dog.

Daniel closed the gap to the open window in three strides. A dark figure disappeared into the trees.

"Izz, stay with Lily and Annie!" He crawled through the opening, dropped to the ground, and took off after the person who'd tried to break in. He glanced behind him, finding Logan coming up on his right. After flashing hand signals at Daniel, Logan slipped into the dark. The navy SEAL stealth hadn't vanished since his brother-in-law retired. He was glad to have the man on his side.

Ducking into the woods, illuminated only by the moonlight, he caught glimpses of movement ahead. Tree bark scraped beneath his boots as he leaped over a fallen log. Adrenaline dulled the sting of briars along his forearms. Whoever this was knew the terrain. Well, so did he, but the guy had a head start.

A flash of movement to the left caught his attention. He veered, nearly slipping on loose gravel as the figure darted across a fence line and vanished behind a stand of cedar. A car engine revved in the distance.

Daniel muttered under his breath and ducked beneath a low-hanging limb. The man had escaped. He strode toward the house, praying Logan had gotten close enough to get a description.

Several minutes later, they met up by the lane. Daniel's frustration bubbled inside, ready to explode. "Anything?"

"No. You?" Logan folded his arms across his chest, his frustration obvious.

He shook his head. "How did they find her?"

"Not a clue. She's been at our house all evening. Why now?"

"Good question."

"We better figure out the answer before someone succeeds in grabbing her." The determination in Logan's tone spoke of a man used to solving the world's problems.

They turned and walked toward the house in silence.

"What if they followed you?" Logan's question hung on the night air.

"It's not my first rodeo. I kept an eye out for a tail and would have noticed. Besides, a car trailing us would have stood out like a neon sign on these dark roads."

"True." Logan got quiet for a moment. "What if they tagged your truck?"

"A tracking device?" Guilt gnawed at him. Why hadn't he considered that? Daniel hated Logan's silence as they approached his truck. "You take that side, I'll look on the other."

He and Logan pulled out their phones and turned on the flashlight app. Dropping to the ground, they searched the vehicle from bumper to bumper.

Daniel's heart stuttered. A small black square clung inside the trailer hitch. "Found it." He wiggled out from under his truck and held the device in his palm. "You were right."

"I hate that I was." Logan dusted off his hands and examined the box. "Lily knows something. It's the only reason whoever this guy is is targeting her. Otherwise, why go to the extreme of sneaking onto the property?"

"Let's go tell the ladies." Daniel folded his fingers over the tracker. Regret washed over him. If he'd only considered the extent the man would go to silence Lily and Annie.

The two men entered the house and moved to the living room. Izzie sat on the recliner, and Annie held Lily on the couch, rocking back and forth. Shadow snuggled against the little girl, his worried eyes never leaving her.

"I take it you didn't catch him." Izzie narrowed her gaze.

Her eyes shifted from Logan to Daniel. "What did you discover?"

He glanced at Lily. He had no intention of scaring the girl further.

"Go ahead. She's asleep," Annie whispered.

Opening his hand, he held out the tracking device. "This was hidden on my truck. The guy we found breaking into Lily's room must have planted it at the rodeo grounds."

"Why? Why try to take or hurt an innocent little girl?" Annie's tone pleaded for answers.

"We don't know. But we all think Lily saw something and can identify the person. And if so, he has to eliminate her before she talks."

"I'm out of my wheelhouse here. Annie, you're the doctor. How do we get her to tell us what she knows?" Izzie asked.

Annie sighed. "We can't. Not until she's ready. This isn't a medical problem. It's a psychological one."

Daniel rubbed the back of his neck. "How do we convince her she's safe?"

"I don't know." Annie kissed her daughter's forehead. "I just don't know."

And there it was. Failure to protect. The inability to keep the most precious person to Annie safe. He couldn't do this again. If another child died… He closed his eyes. He could lose everything—including shattering his heart beyond repair.

"I want you and Lily back on the ranch. It has more security." Daniel left no room for argument.

"I'll get Lily's things. We'll join you. More eyes and ears and all that." Izzie jumped from her seat and scrambled to gather the things she, Logan, and Shadow would need, along with Lily's toys.

"We'll meet you there." Logan clasped Daniel's shoulder. "Take Shadow in case Lily wakes up."

Daniel stared at Annie and the little girl he'd failed to protect. The person who'd tracked them was still out there. He wouldn't make the same mistake again. From here on out, nothing would distract him from safeguarding Lily and her mom. Not even the woman he'd dreamed about for years.

TEN

Annie rubbed the grit from her eyes. Last night had pushed her past her breaking point. The ranch house couch cushions enveloped her, and the coffee's bold aroma hadn't cut through the fog—yet. Her eyes drooped close. It might become a two or three cup day. Fatigue hadn't hit her this hard since medical school. Sleep hadn't come easy last night. And when she dozed, nightmares of knives, blood, Lily's screams, and charging bulls had run like a horror movie in her brain.

"You look like you could use another cup." Daniel lowered onto the recliner across from her and sipped his morning brew.

Odd he'd chosen there to sit and not next to her. She could use the warmth of his hand in hers. The reassurance that everything would work out. "Maybe once I finish this one."

"How's she doing?" He jutted his chin toward her daughter lying on the blanket, petting Shadow.

"Quiet. But that's nothing new." Annie had mentally searched her medical knowledge as she stared at the ceiling last night, but the truth was that nothing except patience and trust would break through the walls of silence.

Daniel fiddled with his coffee mug. He opened his mouth then closed it. His shoulders drooped. "Look, I'm sorry."

She studied him for a moment. What did he have to be sorry for? "Why?"

"For not keeping her safe." He jerked his head toward Lily.

"But you did. You ran after the person who tried to break in."

He shook his head. "That's just it. It never should have happened. It was my truck that the attacker tagged. I'm a deputy. I should have realized. I should have been prepared. But I failed her—and you." Pain rolled off him in waves. The poor guy was drowning in regret.

"Did you put the tracker on your vehicle? Did you tell the guy to abduct or hurt Lily?" She couldn't bring herself to say kill. The idea of her daughter suffering at the mystery man's hands sucked the air from her lungs. She gasped, feeling like a fish flopping on the riverbank.

"Annie?"

Tears pooled on her lashes at the concern in Daniel's tone. Grabbing control of her runaway emotions, Annie blew out a long slow breath. "You did nothing wrong."

"I wish I agreed with you. But the evidence shows the opposite." He dipped his chin, refusing to meet her gaze.

The sweetest softest sound broke the silence.

Annie's eyes shot to her daughter then back to him. "Daniel."

He stared at Lily.

"I don't know what to do, Shadow," Lily whispered.

The dog licked the girl's cheek. A smile flashed on her adorable face and vanished.

"You understand, don't you. But you're brave. You ran him off." Lily snuggled closer to Shadow and wrapped her arms around his furry neck.

"She's talking." A trail of tears streaked Annie's cheeks. She didn't want to interrupt the conversation between girl and dog. "Daniel, keep talking softly."

"I don't know what to say."

"I don't either, but we need her to think we aren't listening." Annie strained to hear Lily's quiet conversation.

Shadow whined in sympathy.

"He's a bad man. He hurt Miss Karly." Lily sniffed. "She hid me in that dark place and told me not to move, but I peeked through a hole. Then Miss Karly screamed. I was so scared, Shadow." She nuzzled the dog, wiping her tears on Shadow's fur.

Daniel's eyes widened, but he lowered his voice. "She can identify Karly's murderer."

Annie nodded. "That's my take on it. My poor baby. She listens to us talk, and I had to tell her about Karly. No wonder she went mute."

Lily continued to whisper to the black Lab, but her one-sided discussion veered to play. A few moments later she stopped talking once again.

"We have to put the pieces together and figure out who is wreaking havoc on the community before he sets his sites on Lily again." Annie's determination spiked. Among her, Daniel, Izzie, and Logan, they had to solve this case before it was too late.

Daniel glanced at Lily and cleared his throat. "I need to… um… I have chores to do." He bolted for the door.

"Daniel, wait."

"I—I can't." His gaze landed on Lily. "She deserves better." With that, he hurried out of the living room. The back door opened and creaked closed.

And just like that, she splintered into pieces. Annie had been there before with Ethan. She'd trusted her ex, and he'd shredded every ounce of belief she'd had in their relationship with a decision he hadn't shared with her until he made the commitment to Doctors Without Borders.

Daniel, on the other hand, had stomped on her heart. She'd

begged Ethan to reconsider—to stay by her side—but she refused to do that with Daniel.

"My son hightailed it out of here like the coyotes were nipping at his heels. You happen to know what set him off?" Miss Hannah sauntered in and plopped onto the couch next to her. "I'm getting too old to chase after young'uns." The woman had arrived early this morning after spending the night with her granddaughter, Lexi.

Annie's chest burned with rejection. "I'm sorry. Lily and I can leave. We've been a lot to deal with. I still have our rental house in town we can go to."

"No. No, honey. That's not what I meant." Hannah's hand covered Annie's thigh. "You can stay as long as you need to. My statement referred to my precocious granddaughter. She's a handful. Not because she's onery, but she keeps me on my toes."

She glanced at Lily. Yeah, she understood that sentiment. "I still feel as though we've worn out our welcome."

"Annie, dear, you've experienced more than anyone should since you arrived in Rollins. I know my kids will put an end to the nonsense, but I'm here for you too."

Those pesky tears flooded her eyes. "Thank you."

"Now that that's settled, tell me why my son stormed out of here."

Daniel had confided in her. She couldn't break that trust. "I…well… Lily started talking to Shadow. I don't think we were supposed to hear, but she admitted to the dog that she saw the bad man."

"Oh, Annie. It's fantastic that she's talking, but it worries me that she knows something and isn't telling you."

"I'm concerned too." She glanced at her daughter, making sure the little one wasn't listening.

They sat in silence a moment, then Hannah smiled. "Nice deflection, by the way."

Of course the woman wouldn't forget her question. Annie sighed. "He's struggling with what happened with Lily last night."

"Honey, you don't have to be so vague. I know my boy is hurting. Has been for years. He wasn't able to protect a child. I know that in my momma's heart. I've seen his reaction to children. I have no idea what happened, but the underlying trauma is there. He loves his niece, Lexi, but he's never once offered to babysit like the other kids have. I've seen him almost panic if asked to be alone with her. Don't take his aversion to Lily personally."

Annie's jaw dropped, and she forced it closed. "How did you know?"

Hannah chuckled. "Those kids of mine think they can hide their problems from me." She tsked playfully. "But a momma knows."

"*That* I understand."

"I'm sure you do. Now, back to Daniel's self-imposed guilt. I don't know specifics, but he came back a different man after his time at the sheriff's academy. He's always carried the persona of class clown, even as a toddler. It got worse when his father left, but when he returned from the academy, the jokester mask to hide his pain became more prominent."

"Why haven't you confronted him?" Annie scrunched her forehead in confusion. If Hannah could have helped him, why hadn't she?

"You'll learn as Lily gets older. Sometimes you just have to pray and hope they'll find someone to open up to if it's not you."

Hadn't she tried that? "He's dealing with the pain of the past, but so am I. He opened up then walked away."

Hannah studied her. "I'm guessing someone left you. Someone you loved?"

Annie deflated. Dropped her and ran was more like it. "He

was a doctor I worked with. I thought I loved him. But it wasn't enough. Just like…" She couldn't say it.

"Like your mom?"

She sucked in a breath. "How did you know?"

"Back in the day when you came to the ranch, you were desperate for love. You never missed an opportunity for a hug."

"It hurts to be the one thrown aside. I've only wanted to feel like I belong."

Hannah patted her leg. "You always have a place in my home and heart, even if my son is being an idiot."

"Hannah!" Annie giggled. "I can't believe you said that."

"I call it like I see it. He has a great thing with you and Lily. He'll come around. Give him time. Now, Payton is a tougher nut to crack." Worry lined Hannah's face, adding to the fine lines in her features.

Annie hadn't reconnected with Payton, Daniel's veterinarian sister, or Cooper, but hopefully she'd see them soon. Assuming Daniel didn't kick her out first. No. She couldn't think like that. She let the quiet settle between her and Hannah for a moment. "What do I do to help Daniel?"

"That, my dear, is a question only you can answer."

Hannah was right. His trauma spoke for him. Annie would support him if he'd let her.

"I better go tend to my chores." The woman stood. "It really is great to have you and your daughter here."

Before the emotion in Annie's throat cleared, Hannah disappeared around the corner.

God, I don't even know where to start. But Lily and Daniel both need you. Please protect them—us. I kinda need you too.

The attacker who was threatening them was still out there. Hiding—watching—waiting.

Daniel stormed into the horse barn. The door swung shut behind him. He stomped over the line of hay bales and kicked the closest one. Dust poofed from the bale, tickling his nose. He sneezed. Stupid move on his part. Now he had hay in his mouth and nose, and a sore toe. His horse, Aspen, whinnied and bobbed his head up and down. He hobbled to his friend, seeking the unconditional love only animals could give.

"Hey, boy."

Aspen nuzzled his neck.

He ran a hand down the paint horse. When the world became tough, Daniel tended to seek comfort from Aspen. And they say girls have special relationships with their horses. Daniel wanted to laugh at the thought, but he couldn't even crack a fake smile.

The horse nibbled on his shirt.

"Stop that. You know better, you big goof." Leave it to him to find a horse with a sense of humor. He closed his eyes and stroked the horse's neck. "I messed up, buddy. I walked out on Annie. It's just she has Lily, and I…I can't go there again. Especially after last night." Daniel swallowed the boulder-sized lump in his throat.

Aspen got more aggressive, searching for the treats Daniel usually kept in his pockets.

"Sorry, boy, I didn't bring anything."

The paint huffed but didn't back away. Finicky little thing.

He ignored Aspen's temper tantrum. "Annie's the woman I waited my whole life for. But then there's Lily." He rested his head against his horse. "Why can't I let it go?"

"Because you won't talk about it and seek out help."

He spun and found his mother with her hands on her hips, standing ten feet away. "We need to buy a bell to hang around your neck. I swear Logan has taught you his navy SEAL stealth tactics."

"Is that right, Mr. Funny Man?" His mom raised a brow, but he didn't miss the smirk she tried to hide.

"Meh. But you are getting better at sneaking up on people."

His mom sat on a hay bale and patted the space next to her. "Come. Sit. Talk."

And just like that he felt like a twelve-year-old boy in trouble again. "Yes, ma'am."

She snorted.

"Okay, I'm here." He sat on the bale of hay and crossed his arms.

"Knock it off, or I'll treat you like a little boy."

He'd admit he sounded like a petulant child, but he had no desire to spill his guts to his mother. He inhaled and bit back a snarky retort. "What would you like to discuss?"

"Why you walked out on Annie. That girl doesn't deserve your attitude. Neither does Lily."

He stiffened. That—right there—was the problem. He knew that, but the screams of the child he couldn't save haunted him every night. Twice a night since Lily came into his life. But last night had sent him over the edge. "You're right. They don't. But I can't be with them."

"Why not?"

He narrowed his gaze at her. "I can't. Just leave it at that."

"Can't or won't?"

"Does it matter?"

She glared at him. "It does and you know it. You walked out on a woman who has had her world ripped out of orbit. You are putting your insecurities ahead of a little girl who needs your expertise and love."

His anger bubbled to eruption level. "You think I don't know that! What else am I supposed to do? Huh, mom? Annie's the woman I want to spend my life with. And Lily—she's incredible. And that's saying something since I've never heard her speak until today. But that's just it. I can't fail them. I can't let another child die because I'm not there to save them. If Lily dies, it will kill Annie. It will shatter what's left of me!" His breath came in ragged bursts.

His mom's arms engulfed him. He lay his head on her shoulder and cried. Cried out his regret. His shame. His pain.

"I'm so sorry, Daniel. I knew you were hurting and expected it had something to do with a child, but I didn't know the little one had died." She ran her hand over his hair like she'd done when he was young. "What happened?"

Even as an independent thirty-year-old, sometimes a man just needed his mother's comfort and wisdom. Through the tears, he sat back and laid out the entire accident to his mom.

"Oh, baby." She wiped her cheeks with her shirtsleeve. "You've lived with this for so long that it's eating you alive."

"I don't know how to move on—how to forget." He'd do almost anything for the nightmares to go away.

"You never forget, but once you trust God to walk you through the process, it becomes bearable. And the pain recedes."

He stared at his mom. "You make is sound so simple."

She gave him a sad smile. "It's not, but what's that old saying? 'The hardest roads lead to the greatest destinations.'"

"Yeah, well, this road is littered with potholes, and I'm in a jalopy with a busted suspension."

His mother's laughter floated in the air. "Oh, son. I love you." She got serious. "Don't throw away a good thing due to fear and stubbornness."

He had fear by the bucketload, but stubborn? Yeah, that too. "Thanks, Mom." Daniel hugged her. "You've given me something to think about."

Hannah patted his cheek. "Sorry to interrupt your man-to-man talk with Aspen. Go on. See what the critter has to say." His mom breezed from the barn, leaving him wrung out from her truth session.

Daniel moved to Aspen's stall and petted the horse's nose. "I guess it's time to man-up and face my fears."

Aspen bobbed his head.

"Thanks a lot there, buddy." Daniel glanced at his watch and took a deep breath. Izzie had texted earlier that morning. She and Logan wanted to go over the case with the new details. His sister should arrive soon. He'd better get back to the house. He strode from the barn a little slower than normal, mulling over what his mother had said.

A while later, he joined Izzie, Logan, and Annie at the formal dining room table. Lily was visible in the living room, playing with Shadow. According to Annie, Lily had stopped talking, but since her breakthrough this morning, she seemed more at ease. Shadow continued his duty, watching over the four-year-old, allowing her to practically climb all over him. Poor dog.

"Now that we're all here…" Izzie squinted at him. No doubt noticing his red eyes.

He gave a slight shake of his head.

She nodded. "Annie said that Lily talked to Shadow this morning and told him a bit about what happened. I think we can all agree that she's a witness. Which makes sense why the guy would come after her. But how would the attacker know she can identify him?"

Annie's face lost all color.

"What is it?"

"While Miss Hannah and I were talking on the phone about her being with Lexi and not at the ranch, I mentioned that Lily had spoken to Shadow. At that point she'd only said a few words, but what if someone heard me?"

"It's not a secret that Lily was traumatized or that she wasn't speaking. The person behind all this could have decided to remove the witness, worried she could identify him." Izzie collected a file from the table.

Annie lifted a shaking hand and pressed her fingertips to her forehead. "You mean my carelessness with my conversation put a target on my daughter."

"You can't think like that. It's not your fault. It's the man who chose to deal in drugs. The man who killed Bonner and Karly." Daniel hated that Annie blamed herself for something out of her control. He froze. Wasn't that what his mom had told him? What he'd done since that horrible day?

Izzie pursed her lips. "I'm sorry, Annie. My bluntness tends to get me in trouble."

"You spoke your mind. There's nothing wrong with that. Can we forget about it and focus on finding the guy who's after Lily?"

"And you." Daniel didn't want her to forget that the danger applied to her as well.

Logan cleared his throat. "Grace approved me working with y'all. As if there was any doubt, but it's official. Your case is in GracePoint Security's books and includes all the support that comes with it. I've run background checks on the carnies and vendors, focusing on the ones in Bonner's photos. Carnival workers Wade Culter and Dustin Bragg. We crossed Bragg off the suspect list, but Culter's another story. I pulled up his bank records. The man has large amounts of cash deposited in his account a couple times a month, and it doesn't come from his carnival job."

"Keep him on the list." Izzie tapped her pen against her lips. The woman tended to work better with pen and paper. Someday, he'd get his sister into this century. "What about the vendors and rodeo personnel?"

"That's where things get interesting in general. The rodeo community appears clean." Logan shrugged. "I mean, there are a few fights and traffic tickets and such, but overall, things look good. Which is amazing after what happened over the past year. I did a deep dive on the vendors, with an extra focus on Clayton Rusk, the feed and grain vendor, since Bonner had multiple pictures of his trailer, and Conor Murray, who owns

Canyon Ridge Gear. There are images of Murray's setup, plus he found Karly's body."

"While y'all recovered from last night, I was busy this morning interviewing Murray and Rusk. Conor Murray said he stumbled upon Karly's body, and I believe him."

"What was he doing behind the barn?" Daniel wasn't buying the happy accident.

Izzie smirked. "Apparently, he planned to inhale some wacky weed."

A deep belly laugh rumbled from Daniel. "Bet he hated to admit that to the sheriff."

"Yeah." Izzie dragged out the word. "He wasn't happy to confess that in front of law enforcement, but bottom line, he did."

"Did you have an opportunity to talk with Clayton Rusk?"

"I did. He allowed me to search his grain stock. Guess what I found."

"Drugs," Annie offered.

"Ding, ding, ding. Give the woman a prize."

"Then it's Clayton? Why didn't you say so in the first place?" Daniel hated playing this game with his sister. He wanted answers.

"Not so fast. Clayton was shocked. No one is that good of an actor. He is as he appears—a good guy. That leaves his employees. I want more info on those two. I'm not ruling anyone out yet. If Clayton didn't put the drugs in his supplies, I want to know who did. There could be multiple people involved. I'd be negligent in my duties if I focused on one person or method."

"True. Sorry."

Izzie nodded her acceptance of his apology.

"I'm still waiting for details on those two. But what I did discover solidifies this entire case." Logan eyes shifted from one person to the next.

"Stop with the suspense, dude. Spit it out." Daniel wanted to throttle his brother-in-law.

Logan glanced at Izzie, and she nodded for him to continue. "After talking to the medical examiner and the lab, reviewing all the suspected related deaths, some of the fentanyl funneled through the region is hospital grade and some is street. Izzie and I talked with the DEA. We are now 100 percent sure the fentanyl pipeline runs through San Antonio." Logan's gaze landed on Annie.

Annie's body deflated. "Dr. Pope."

"It appears that way. The DA down there is taking a closer look. He's also contacting his counterparts in Houston and Dallas. So far, we've discovered this thing runs from Mexico, where the street drugs come from, through major cities for the medical grade. The DEA is re-examining what they have, but with the new information, it looks as though the connections to the hospitals are solid."

"Do you think Dr. Pope is behind the attacks here?" Annie asked.

The creases in Izzie's forehead deepened. "I think he's a cog in the bigger picture. However, you did put a spotlight on him and the drugs he stole from the hospital."

"Have you heard from Dr. Gregory?" Logan asked.

"No. He hasn't been in contact with me other than the early text messages, confirming Dr. Pope is still in San Antonio." Annie sighed.

"So it's possible Dr. Pope made his way to Rollins." Daniel mulled over the conversation. Something didn't sit right with him, but he couldn't figure out what. "Are we still thinking one crime? Annie's interference with Bonner's attack put her in the crosshairs of his killer, and Lily and Karly witnessed this man do something he didn't want discovered?"

"It's either that or we have two or three crimes." Izzie rubbed her temples. "What does your gut say, Daniel?"

He refused to give a quick snarky answer. The entire case smelled like wet manure. "Gut reaction, we have one case—one crime."

"We're in agreement then." Izzie slumped in her seat. "My brain hurts."

"Let me finish with Clayton Rusk's employees. One loads and drives the truck. The other is administrative and works all the purchases." Logan typed notes into his laptop. "Once I have that information, Izzie and I will dive deeper into our current suspects and any connections to the larger city hospitals we missed."

"Keep us up to date on what you find out. My guess is it's one of the vendors or their employees. What easier way to slip the drugs into the shipment and bring them in unnoticed." Daniel stood. "Annie and I need to get to the rodeo grounds."

"Lily's coming with me. I don't like her being there, but no one's available to watch her again." Annie gathered her coffee mug.

"Sorry about that, Annie. I have physical research I have to do today on another case that I can't put off any longer." Logan rubbed the back of his neck. "But keep Shadow with you."

"I didn't mean it like that, Logan. I don't expect you to be my constant babysitter. And are you sure you don't want to keep your dog?" Annie asked. Apparently, she'd clued in to Logan's lack of sleep as well.

"Positive. Lily needs him more than I do."

"Thank you. She'll appreciate that." Annie moved to the archway and faced Daniel. "I'll get her packed up, then we can go."

He nodded. When she left the room, he spun. "Izzie, this has to end."

"Bro, I'm trying."

He dipped his chin to his chest. "I know. It's just that..."

"You don't have to say it. I get it." Her eyes shifted to Logan.

"Yeah, I guess you do." Izzie and Logan had experienced their own horrors not long ago.

"You love her, don't you?" Izzie's question startled him.

He never dreamed the day would arrive when he talked about his love life with his sister. Did he love Annie? Yeah, he did. But with Lily in the picture, could he put the past to rest? "It's complicated."

"Then uncomplicate it. She's good for you, and you her. Besides, Lily needs a father. You'd be great at that."

They'd agree to disagree on that point. One thing he knew for certain. He had to stop a madman before it was too late and he lost them both.

ELEVEN

Documents logged from last night's rodeo injuries and an order request sent to Keats, Annie stood in the doorway to the exam room. Lily sat on a blanket in the main office with Shadow next to her. The dog hadn't left her side since they arrived a couple of hours ago. She'd have to remember to take him out for a potty break soon. But until then, she planned to reorganize the supplies to her liking.

Her cell phone rang. She pulled it from her pocket and answered without looking at the caller ID. "Dr. Anderson."

"Hi, Annie. Is everything okay?" Daniel's concern flowed over the line.

"We're fine. Lily's playing, and I'm prepping to make this space my own."

"Good. I feel bad that I can't be there. I'd planned to stop by, but I've been in meetings with Donovan Keats for the past hour or so. If you need me, I'm in the arena going over safety and security measures."

"Thanks, but we're fine. The door's locked, and I haven't advertised that I'm here."

"Good. I'll check in soon." He disconnected the call.

Annie exhaled. "Well, at least he isn't being a jerk and seemed genuinely concerned." Great, she was talking to herself again. It bothered her that Daniel had pulled away earlier that morning, but when he'd returned from the barn, he'd seemed conflicted. She'd heed Miss Hannah's advice and allow him the time to wrestle with his guilt and regret. But the man gave her serious whiplash. What had gotten into him? She glanced at her daughter and closed her eyes. It was all due to Lily and the thwarted abduction. Who was she kidding? Every synonym for kidnapped wouldn't change the fact that the man had planned to kill her daughter. No wonder Daniel had shut down.

She shook off her train of thought. "All right, girl. Get busy." Annie opened the cabinet drawers and started reorganizing.

A whimper came from the front room.

She rushed in and found Lily cowering in the corner. Shadow stood at the door. A deep growl rumbled from the dog.

"Sweetie, what's wrong?"

Lily pointed to the window. "Bad man."

Stunned that her daughter spoke, it took a second for Annie's brain to connect the dots. "You saw the bad man through the window?"

Lily nodded.

"Is he the one who hurt Karly?"

Lily shrunk in on herself even more, if that were possible. "Yes," the little girl whispered.

The doorknob jiggled, then a thump against the door made her jump.

Annie's mind raced through the options to keep her daughter safe. Calling Daniel ranked at the top, but she had to get Lily away from the front room and the person trying to get in first. She grabbed Lily's hand and pulled her into the exam room. "Shadow, come."

The dog followed her command. She shut and locked the door behind them.

She pulled out her phone to dial Daniel's number when the

front door splintered open. Abandoning the idea of calling, she crouched in front of Lily. "Sweetie, listen to me. Listen closely. I'm going to boost you through the window back here. You're going to run to the big arena over there." She pointed to the grandstands through the glass. "I'm going to climb out behind you. We need to find Mr. Daniel and tell him about the bad man."

Big, scared eyes stared at her.

"You can do it. I know you can." The rattle of the interior door intensified and the thumps got louder, along with Shadow's terrifying growl. "Lily, remember the tomato and cucumber that sang about how big God is?"

Her daughter nodded.

"Sing that while you run to Daniel. Please." She hated begging Lily, but both their lives relied on escaping. "I'm coming out the window behind you, but you have to take off as soon as your feet hit the ground."

"Okay, Momma."

Annie almost cried. "Come on." She slid the window open. The door cracked. A few more hits and the guy would break into the exam room. She had to get Lily out of there. Lifting her daughter up, she kissed her on the cheek. "Go. Get help. I love you."

"I love you too, Momma." The moment Lily was on the ground she took off running.

Shadow barked and growled behind her.

Annie lifted her leg to crawl out the window when the door crashed in. A large hand grabbed the back of her shirt and yanked her down. She hit the floor, and her hair fell across her face, blocking her vision.

No matter what happened to her, Lily had gotten away. Her only hope now was a scared four-year-old.

Lord, let her make it and be able to communicate with Daniel. I know I'm asking a lot. Please, help her.

"Shut him up or he's dead."

No. Not Logan's dog. "Shadow, leave it," she croaked.

The dog stopped but snarled. He wasn't happy.

"Good. Now, where'd you send the brat?"

Wait. She knew that voice. Annie swiped the hair from her face and got a good look at the man who pointed the barrel of a gun at Shadow.

"You? I trusted you!" Annie's heart shattered. "Why?"

"You got my top supplier arrested. Although maybe I should thank you. He was an idiot."

She stared at her mentor, Dr. Gregory, the man who she considered a father figure. "Did you kill your own niece?"

"Me? Technically no. But she saw me hand off drugs to Grant and threatened to turn me in. I couldn't let her get away and tell the cops. Karly had to die. My poor sister's beside herself with grief." Dr. Gregory actually looked pained by that statement. "But what's done is done. She'll get over it."

"No, she won't." How could Annie not have seen what her mentor really was?

"Either way, it's too late now. And as for you, you destroyed this part of the fentanyl pipeline. And from what my people are telling me, you've alerted the DEA, and they are closing in." His eyes hardened. "You'll pay for that."

Annie shuddered. No wonder Lily went mute. For all intents and purposes, her *grandfather* hurt Karly. *Please let Lily tell Daniel about Gregory.*

"Enough of this. Lock the mutt in the bathroom." He jabbed the gun toward the dog.

"Come on, Shadow." The dog didn't budge. "Shadow, come," she said with more force.

Shadow's black eyes never left Dr. Gregory, but he obeyed. Once she shut the dog in the bathroom, she turned to her onetime friend. "Now what?"

"Now we go for a walk." He grabbed her arm and yanked.

Pressing the barrel into her back, he guided her outside. "Don't make a sound or I'll start shooting. I don't care who dies, but I think you do."

She nodded and obeyed as he led her through the fairgrounds and toward the woods beyond.

Other lives might have been saved, but this was it for her. This is how it would end. Her only hope was a four-year-old who struggled to speak out of fear.

God, You're in control. I trust You. If the worst happens, please help Daniel forgive himself, and give Lily a long, happy life.

For the first time in her life, a sense of peace accompanied by unconditional love washed over her.

Sweat and fine particles of hay glued Daniel's shirt to his back. The temperatures had risen and so had the humidity. Another sticky day in Texas. Under normal circumstances, he wouldn't care, but the weight of the air mimicked his mood. He'd hurt Annie. He hadn't intended to, but the nightmares and regrets hung heavy on his shoulders. It was like the world wanted to drive him to the ground. And then there was Lily. What did he do about her? He didn't hate kids. In fact, before the academy and that dreaded day, he'd wanted a passel of them. Now—he didn't trust himself to be alone with a child. His mom's words slammed into him. Okay, so maybe he did need to deal with his issues before he died a grumpy old curmudgeon.

"Daniel, did you hear Clayton?" Izzie jolted him from his thoughts.

"Sorry." He glanced around, confirming there was no one listening to the small group gathered near the steer pens. They'd moved from the arena when workers had shown up. Donovan and the feed and grain vendor, Clayton, had joined him and Izzie.

She narrowed her gaze and studied him then turned to the other men. “Bro, you need to pay attention.”

“Sorry, Clayton. This whole situation has me out of sorts. Go ahead.”

“I did some digging around my office after we talked. My driver, Kurt, is clean. Or at least I think so. But my office administrative assistant, Grant Knox—not so much. I brought printouts of our purchases. The numbers don’t match. I compared the official spreadsheets to the purchase order Grant gives Kurt. There are always a few extra bags on each delivery.”

“I’d say we found the person on this end of the pipeline.” Daniel scratched his jaw. “Izzie, can we pick him up right now for questioning?”

“Normally, I’d say no, that we need to have our evidence airtight. But RPD pulled him over this morning for running a red light.” Izzie chuckled. “God has a sense of humor.”

“Why? Did He put a neon sign over Grant’s head saying Killer?”

“Very funny, Daniel. But no. Since Clayton called with his discovery, we had reason to search his car.” Izzie took a dramatic pause.

And here Daniel thought he was the funny one in the family. “Knock it off, sis. What happened?”

“The smoking gun. Or in this case the bloody knife and a nice little supply of fentanyl.”

“Are you kidding me?” He laughed. *Thank You, God.*

“We’re still comparing blood samples to Deputy Bonner, but Grant’s already acting squirrely. He’s in custody as we speak. I think he’ll end up spilling his secrets before long.”

Daniel’s shoulder sagged in relief. “Unless proved otherwise, we have Bonner and Karly’s murderer and Annie’s attacker.”

“It looks that way.”

Something bothered him, and he couldn't quite put his finger on it. It all came back to Izzie's statement about Grant.

"What's eating you, Daniel?" Izzie rested her hands on her hips.

"If he's that easily influenced and on the edge of talking, how can he be the brains of this mess?"

"He has a point." Donovan Keats, the rodeo director who had been silent up to that point, chimed in.

"You think he's the lackey and someone else is the brains?"

"Think about it." He lifted his cowboy hat and wiped his forehead. "He escapes from the lake and runs. I'll even buy the attack at the hospital. It was crude and not well thought out. He aimed to kill Bonner, not Annie until she intervened. And from what y'all said, I'm not sure he has the smarts or guts to pull off something this organized."

"I've dealt with him on occasion and can't argue with that," Donovan said.

"So, another person pulling the strings?" Clayton sighed. "I'll help y'all clean my side of this ugly barn, but I can't help you with the other side. Listen, I need to get back to work. Let me know if I can do anything else."

"Thanks, Clayton." Daniel shook the man's hand.

"Know of anyone who needs a job?" The man chuckled, shook his head, and meandered toward the barn.

"Give me a second. I'm going to check on Annie." He pulled out his phone and placed the call. The phone rang multiple times then flipped to voicemail. He hung up.

Izzie placed her hand on his shoulder. "What's wrong?"

"She's not picking up." His stomach knotted. Why in the world hadn't she answered? She'd promised to stay locked in her office.

"Maybe she left her phone on silent or turned down her ringer."

"I doubt it. But the other day her phone died. Maybe that's

it. But that doesn't make sense either. It would go straight to voicemail if that happened."

"Mr. Daniel!" A soft frantic voice drifted from the horse barn. "Mr. Daniel!" A cute pint-size blonde dashed outside, her wide eyes searching.

"Lily?" He jogged toward the little girl.

She flung herself into his arms. "Mr. Daniel." Tears poured down her tiny cheeks, wetting his shirt.

"Honey, what's wrong?" He held tight but scanned the area for Annie. "Where's your momma?"

"He came to Momma's office." The little girl sobbed.

"Who, sweetie?"

Izzie and Donovan joined them, looking on anxiously for answers. Probably as stunned as he was that Annie's daughter spoke.

"Lily, honey, can you tell me what happened?" He tried to pull back a bit to see her face, but her arms tightened around his neck. "Wait. Where's Shadow?"

The little girl's hiccupped sobs came harder and faster.

He stood and lifted her in his arms, holding her close. Her tiny body trembled. *What do I do?* he mouthed to Izzie.

Just keep talking. You're doing great, she mouthed back.

Right. His nerves were humming at the idea of Annie being in trouble. Not to mention his heart had roped itself to Lily, and he never wanted to let go. But he needed answers.

"Lily, I know it's hard, but can you be brave and tell me where your momma is?" He ran his hand up and down her back, hoping to comfort her.

She sniffed and lifted her head but didn't remove her arms from his neck. "She made me climb out the window so the bad man wouldn't hurt me. She was supposed to come with me."

Now they were getting somewhere. "The bad man came into the exam room?"

"No." She sniffed again.

"I'm sorry, Lily, I don't understand." He now understood the old saying "like pulling teeth."

She huffed—literally huffed at him. He'd laugh if his nerves weren't ready to snap. "Where was the bad man?"

"Trying to get in the second door."

"And Shadow? Where was he?"

"Growling."

Daniel slowly put the pieces together.

"Let me see if I have it right. The bad man tried to get into the exam room and Shadow growled at him. Your momma told you to go through the window and find me?" Man, he hoped he had it right. Talking to a scared four-year-old was like putting a puzzle together without the picture.

She nodded.

"Come on." Izzie strode through the barn on a mission.

Daniel followed his sister, carrying Lily tucked against him. He stood back at a safe distance and let his sister breech the building. But he was ready to pass the little girl off to Donovan if Izzie required help.

Shadow ran out of the building, followed by Izzie. She sighed and holstered her weapon. "She's gone. I found Shadow shut in the bathroom. Let me tell you, he wasn't happy about it either."

Who had Annie? Lily's words clicked in his head. "Hold on. Lily said he came into the office."

"You think she knows who the man is?" Izzie whispered.

He knelt and sat Lily on her feet. Gently grasping her shoulders, he ducked his head and peered up at her. "Did you know the man who came after your momma?"

The little girl's gaze dropped to the ground. Her lips pinched together.

Shadow trotted over and licked her face, comforting her the only way the dog could.

"Honey, I know it's scary, but Momma needs your help."

She stayed quiet, but he refused to rush her even if he wanted to scream at her to tell him.

He brushed a hand down her hair, cupped her cheek, and waited.

The little girl swallowed—hard. "I thought he was our friend." Tears rolled unchecked off her chin.

"Who, Lily?"

"Dr. Gregory."

Well, dip him in honey and unleash the fire ants—he didn't see that coming. "Why do you think he'll hurt your momma?"

"'Cause he hurt Miss Karly." Lily broke down and bawled.

He tucked the child under his chin and held her tight to his chest. No wonder Lily had refused to talk. The person who promised to protect them had betrayed them.

"You did good, Lily. You did good."

"I texted Mom. She's pulling into the rodeo grounds as we speak. She'll be here in a couple of minutes to take Lily. One of GracePoint's security guards will stay with them while we scour the area for Annie." Izzie's hand rested on Lily's back. "We will find her and bring her home."

He'd made a promise like that once, and it hadn't turned out so well. But he understood Izzie's determination.

"She's right, Lily. We *will* find your momma." Or he'd die trying to ease Lily's heartache.

A few moments later, he passed Lily off to his mother. After giving final instructions to the guard, he and Izzie took off to search for Annie.

"Where is she?" Daniel's body hummed with adrenaline. He couldn't have found her only to lose her again.

"I don't know, but we can't give up. Best guess is either Gregory got her to a car and took off or he absconded with her into the woods."

"I think I prefer the woods over leaving the park." Daniel regretted leaving Annie and Lily alone. He'd thought they'd be safe locked in her office. Another mistake to add to the many when it came to her.

"You really love her, don't you?"

"I do." No need to hide his feelings. They had taken center stage. Only a fool would be oblivious.

"What about Lily?" Izzie examined hiding places in the cattle barn they'd entered a moment ago.

Daniel showed several 4-H members a picture of Annie, but no one had seen her. "What do you mean?"

"Come on, Daniel. I hired you. Even though you're my brother, you don't think I checked with your academy field officer? He told me about the accident."

He froze. "All this time you knew about that?"

She nodded and nudged him to continue through the barn. "I did. I've witnessed the way you let everyone else take care of Lexi. Then Lily came along, and you kept your distance. Well, as much as possible. Something happened that changed your attitude toward the little girl, then you flip-flopped again. But back there? You could have passed her off to me, but you didn't."

He snorted. "Yeah, Mom happened."

"I've been on the receiving end of that hit and run." Izzie scanned the area one last time before they moved to the next section of the fairgrounds.

"And how'd that work out for you?" Daniel was truly curious if his mom had helped his sister.

"Well, let's see. I got over myself and married Logan." She shrugged. "So, I guess you could say Mom was right. But please don't tell *her* that."

Daniel chuckled. "My lips are sealed." He turned serious again. "I can't deny I'm still living with regrets from that accident, but Lily…" How did he describe his feelings for her? "Let's just say that I don't want to lose either one of them."

"Good." Izzie slapped him on the back. "Let's talk to those

people over there." She stopped an older couple and flashed a picture of Annie. "Have you seen this woman? She was separated from her daughter and we're trying to locate her."

"Oh, that's horrible. That poor baby." The woman placed a hand to her chest and studied the image of Annie. "Hank, didn't we see her over near the back of the sheep barn a bit ago?"

The older gentleman stroked his chin. "Yes, dear, I think we did. She and the fella with her seemed to be quite cozy."

"Thank you. We appreciate your help." Daniel shook the man's hand. "Come on, Izz. Let's go."

They quickened their pace, their cowboy boots kicking up dust as they hurried to the back section of the fairgrounds.

This time nothing would stop him from protecting the woman he loved and reuniting her with her daughter. He couldn't deny it any longer. The little girl had wormed her way into his heart.

TWELVE

Annie's mentor, Dr. Todd Gregory, shoved the steel barrel of his gun into her side for the hundredth time. Okay, maybe not a hundred, but too many to count. Enough to leave a bruise the size of Texas under her ribs. He jabbed again, harder this time. Her muscles clenched, and she bit back a whimper.

"Move." He yanked her arm.

Her boots tangled in the underbrush of the woods beyond the fairgrounds. She stumbled, knees buckling, but caught herself before face-planting in the dirt.

Had Lily found Daniel? Or had she asked too much of her four-year-old daughter? Tears pricked her eyes.

God, whatever happens to me, please keep my baby safe.

"Why are you doing this, Todd?" Her voice cracked.

"Shut up!" He released her arm and placed a call on his cell phone. But the weapon held at point-blank range kept her from pulling away. He hit End.

"As if it'll make a difference. You plan to kill me." Annie clenched her teeth. Fear had come and gone, leaving her body trembling with anger. The dried leaves crunched beneath her feet, adding to her fury.

He let go of her arm and tried the call again. When whoever he'd called didn't answer, he jabbed the button like it offended him. Words that would put a sailor to shame spewed from his mouth. The behavior was odd for Gregory. But then again, she really didn't know the man. He'd lied to her, letting her think he cared.

Her fury reached DEFCON 1 level. Until that moment, panic had taken over. But now—fight mode had settled deep inside her. Her gaze scanned the trees. When the time came, she'd escape his grip. Her life and Lily's depended on Daniel finding her before it was too late. Giving him time became her top priority.

"What's wrong? Your grunt not answering to do your dirty work?" Provoking him might not be the best idea, but she couldn't resist.

"I said shut up!" He pushed her in front of him and jammed the gun into her back.

Step by step they moved farther into the woods. An opening to run would present itself. It had to. "How did you get into serving death?"

"You don't know when to keep your mouth closed, do you?"

"I'm inquisitive. So, sue me." She ducked under a low-hanging branch, giving her an idea.

"Medical school and malpractice insurance is expensive. Then there's my wife who spends money faster than I can make it."

"So, it's all about money?"

Todd laughed. "What else is there?"

"People's lives. The doctor's motto of doing no harm. You were trained to save lives, not destroy them."

Gregory grunted. "That's very high and mighty of you."

The man had become someone Annie didn't know. Had she ever known him? "Pope was helping you, wasn't he?"

"He had his usefulness as a dealer in San Antonio until he messed up."

"Then why did you help me get him arrested?"

"Simple. He became a liability when he started using."

The air, heavy with heat and humidity, pressed down on her. "What about me? Lily? Did we ever mean anything to you?"

"Believe it or not, I was happy you'd found another job. I didn't want to hurt you. But then you had to go and get a job here in Rollins. Of all the places in the world, you had to come here."

"Sorry to mess up your plans." Annie slipped and slammed her hand into the trunk of a tree, slicing into her palm. "Why send your goon after me?"

"Because you had to go and save Deputy Bonner, the little fink. My man saw him talk to you and give you something. We couldn't have you spilling the beans, now, could we? Of course, I didn't know *you* were the doctor he talked about until I saw Lily."

"Why try to hurt her? She's just a kid."

"Lily saw me when Karly stumbled upon me completing a transaction. I knocked her to the ground to keep her from running, but she escaped and hid the kid before I could stop her. When I found Karly, I had my employee *handle* the situation. I searched for Lily until they discovered Karly's body. I heard that she went mute and thought I was in the clear. Then I learned she'd said a few words. And we all know that's the precursor for her to speak again."

Shock rendered Annie speechless, giving her a new respect for Lily's trauma response. Gathering her composure, she released a shaky breath. "So what? You're going to kill her?"

Todd shrugged. "I'll do what I have to do to protect my business."

Annie's stomach dropped. The man had no heart. If she didn't get away from him soon, she never would. She wouldn't be able to tell Daniel what she'd learned so he could protect Lily.

Eyes on the ground, avoiding tripping hazards, a plan formed in her mind.

God, please let me pull this off. If it doesn't work, I'll see You soon.

Ask much as she craved to be in His presence, Lily gave her the extra fight to live. Mustering her courage, Annie slowly inhaled.

There—ahead—her opportunity. She willed her heart rate to slow and concentrated on her target. A low-hanging branch and a thick three-foot stick lay in her path.

A few more steps. She could do this. She had to if she had any hopes of staying alive.

Todd mumbled a few choice words. "That idiot. Where is he?"

Annie felt the gun ease from her back. The space between the barrel and her body gave her the encouragement she needed. She pretended to trip and fall. The branch blocked Todd from grabbing her right away. Hands on the stick, she twisted and swung. The piece of wood connected with Todd's face.

Her mentor's head snapped to the side. He stumbled backward. His finger jerked, and the gun went off.

Pain seared her upper arm, and tears blurred her vision. She had no clue if Todd had fallen to the ground or if he'd shoot her again, but it didn't matter. Determination fueled her. She staggered to her feet and lurched forward. Blood trickled down her arm and dripped from her fingertips. Roots tripped her, but she refused to give up.

She dodged trees and brush, staying ahead of him. Where was the edge of the woods? Sobs caught in her throat. Her lungs burned, and the gash in her arm throbbed.

A gunshot rang out.

Annie screamed. This was it. The day she'd meet Jesus face-to-face.

A gunshot had spiked Daniel's heart rate, and he'd poured on speed. Getting to Annie became his sole focus. Gun held at his side, he pressed deeper into the woods behind the sheep barn with Izzie step for step beside him. Tangled roots threatened to keep him from his objective. Stopping Gregory and protecting Annie. The thunk of their boots on the packed dirt forest floor and puffs of air from exertion echoed in his ears. But it was the blood-chilling question that pinballed in his mind. Had Todd Gregory killed Annie before he could save her?

Izzie's hand shot out and gripped his arm. "Daniel," she whispered.

He jolted to a stop. Irritation bubbled inside. Voice low, he demanded, "What is it?"

"Look." She pointed to the ground. Blood drops spotted the dried leaves.

The crimson dots churned his stomach. He swallowed so he didn't lose his lunch. "Annie?"

"That's my guess. But it's a minor wound. Not enough to be life-threatening."

He gritted his teeth. "I don't care how much it is. She's hurt."

"We'll get to her, but you have to be smart."

"Fine. You take the lead." Letting Izzie call the shots was the right thing to do. His judgment was compromised. Smashed to pieces by his heart. Daniel let go of the lighthearted mask he'd worn for years and pinned Izzie with a glare. "But you better not let Annie die."

"She's our top priority. I promise." Izzie stared back and lifted an eyebrow. Her way of asking if they were good.

He nodded. He trusted his sister. But relinquishing command when Annie's life was at stake took everything in him.

"Slow down. Go in quiet. We want the element of surprise." Izzie motioned for him to proceed.

Moving with as much stealth as possible through the dried leaves and twigs, they followed the blood drops. He fought the urge to call out for Annie. Instead, he focused on clues to Annie's whereabouts.

Voices drifted through the foliage.

Izzie held up a fist, stopping him in his tracks.

"You shouldn't have done that." That had to be Gregory.

"Did you expect me to give up and allow you to shoot me?"

Daniel's shoulders sagged in relief. He'd recognize that sass anywhere. Annie was alive.

The argument floated through the air. If Daniel had to guess, Gregory and Annie were playing a game of cat and mouse. Time to spring a trap on the cat.

Izzie tapped him on the shoulder and pointed to the left.

He dipped his chin in acknowledgment and veered left, ducking beneath a low-hanging branch while Izzie flanked right. Sweat gathered on his palm. Switching the weapon to his nondominant hand, he swiped the moisture on his pant leg before returning the grip to his dominant one.

A deep laugh startled Daniel. He crouched and peered through the shrub.

Gregory had his fingers twisted in her hair, yanking her toward him.

Daniel bit back the demand to let her go. *Get a grip, man. Do your job or else Annie will die.*

Unlike the child in the fatal accident, if he used his brain, Annie would live. He no longer questioned his abilities. He truly believed he could—would—save her.

God, show me the way.

Gregory flung Annie to the ground. Her hands and knees skidded on the forest floor a few yards away from where Daniel watched the scene play out.

"Get up!" The man clutched the neck of Annie's shirt and forced her to stand. Sunlight trickled through the trees, reflecting off the gun barrel aimed at Annie's temple.

Tears streaked a path through the dirt on her cheeks.

To pull this off, he had to quietly get Annie's attention. He knew Izzie would take over if the pair moved closer to her. But right now, the rescue was on Daniel.

He pushed through the tangled limbs and brush. Not much. Just enough for Annie to notice him.

Her eyes connected with his and widened.

Bingo. He winked at her for encouragement as Gregory continued to belittle Annie about her caring heart. Daniel raked his gaze around the tree-filled area. There. Across from his hiding spot, Izzie lifted her chin, giving him the go-ahead.

He ran the different scenarios through his mind. Each had the potential to end badly, but he couldn't wait any longer. In the few minutes he'd listened to Gregory, the man had lost more and more of reality.

God, don't let me make a mistake.

Now, how did he communicate his plan with Annie? He caught her eye and shifted his downward with a quick dip of his head.

The gun pressed deeper into the side of her head. She whimpered but maintained her gaze on him. She blinked once.

Good girl. Pulling in a lungful of air, he lifted his weapon and waited for Annie to do her part.

"How dare you treat me like this! I thought we were friends!" Anger spewed from Annie. She twisted, catching Gregory off guard, and dropped to the ground.

Daniel rushed from the brush. "Police!"

Gregory whipped his gun toward him.

Both men fired at the same time.

A searing burn ripped through Daniel's shoulder. The impact spun him, sending him sprawling on the ground. Pain exploded, blinding him as he fought to stay conscious. He rolled and clamped a hand over the wound. Blood pooled beneath his fingers. Staring at the sky peeking through the trees, he gasped, breath catching in his throat. His vision blurred. He struggled to clear the haze.

"Daniel!" Izzie's shout shot adrenaline through his veins.

Staggering to his feet, he stumbled to where Annie's mentor lay on the ground. Daniel cleared the weapon from the man's reach. "Izzie, secure Gregory!"

"On it. But I don't think he's moving for a while. You hit your target, dear brother."

Daniel blew out puffs of air, getting the pain under control. Gregory lay crumpled on the ground. Blood oozed from his chest.

"You didn't hit his heart, but he needs a medic—fast." Izzie wadded up the button-down shirt she wore over her tank top and pressed it against Gregory's wound.

"I'll call it in." He fumbled with his phone one-handed and called dispatch, requesting medical. With his sister dealing with the *good* doctor. Daniel swayed on wobbly legs to Annie's side.

She lay face down, unmoving. Her hair covering her face.

The cracks in his heart webbed outward. *Please, God, don't let it end like this.* He dropped to his knees. "Annie?"

Shaking from fear—or shock, he had no idea—he placed his finger from his free hand to the pulse point on her neck. Too unsteady to feel the light thump against her skin, he sat back and opened and closed his fist.

Before he could check again, Annie stirred. She rolled her head to the side. "Is it safe?" Her whispered words brought tears to his eyes.

"Gregory's in Izzie's custody. Are you okay?" He brushed the strands of hair from her cheek.

She nodded. "As long as Todd goes to jail and never gets out, I'll be fine." Annie's gaze lifted to him. She gasped. "Daniel, your shoulder." On all fours, she crawled to his side. "Let me look."

"Not gonna lie, it hurts like I've been struck by lightning."

"I don't doubt it." She pulled the material away from the gunshot wound. Checked both the front and back of his shoulder. "It's a through and through. That's a good thing. No bullet to remove. And from first glance, it looks like it missed any major arteries or bones. Although I'm not 100 percent sure. Either way, it doesn't appear serious." She gave him a sad smile. "Even though it hurts like your arm's going to fall off."

"Yeah, that about covers how it feels."

The pain had morphed from hot poker status to an intense throb, clearing his thoughts. He took in Annie's scrapes and bruises. His gaze landed on her bicep. "Is that gash from a bullet?"

She glanced down. "I didn't move fast enough. But the bleeding has pretty much stopped."

"Annie." He didn't recognize the whiny tone coming from his lips.

"Relax, mister. I'm okay. You're alive. Lily talked. And Todd is in custody. My prayers are answered."

"Yo, where are you guys?" Paramedic Noah's voice rang out.

"Follow my voice. And hurry up, would you?" Izzie yelled.

Harper and Noah broke through the trees, loaded down with medical duffels and the medical rescue basket.

Izzie motioned with her head since her hands were otherwise busy putting pressure on Gregory's injury. "Over here. I can't stop the bleeding."

Noah knelt across from Izzie and started treating the drug-dealing doctor.

Harper joined Daniel and Annie. "I can see you aren't exactly injury free."

"Harper, you do have a way of understating things." He rolled his eyes.

"Come on, big guy, let's take a look and give you something

to take the edge off. If I'm satisfied, we'll let the emergency room docs deal with you."

Annie chuckled. "I like you, Harper."

"Back at ya, Doc." Harper pointed at Annie. "And by the way, you're next."

With him and Annie in good hands, and Gregory no longer an immediate concern, assuming the man lived, the tension in Daniel's body melted away.

Thank You, God, for protecting Annie. I want a future with her and Lily, and I won't be able to do that without Your help. I'm ready to put the past behind me.

THIRTEEN

The afternoon sun filtered through the large windows in the living room of the ranch house, illuminating dust motes dancing in the air. Annie sat on the leather couch. Lily's small body was in her arms, curled against her. She tucked her nose in Lily's hair and breathed in the sweet watermelon smell from the shampoo Miss Hannah had supplied. After Annie and Daniel had spent the night in the hospital due to their injuries, the ranch house had become Annie's safe haven. She couldn't thank Miss Hannah enough for fighting the hospital staff to allow Lily permission to stay in her room. The agony from the idea of being away from her daughter hurt worse than her list of injuries. The dull ache in Annie's arm and blossoming bruises on her hip and back were reminders of the close calls she'd experienced.

"Doing okay?" Daniel sat next to her. He clutched Lily's leg like if he let go, the little girl would vanish.

She tightened her hold on her daughter. "I'm perfect." Annie had everything she'd ever wanted. Her daughter in her arms, and Daniel by her side. "How's your shoulder?"

He shrugged and grimaced. Adjusting the black sling, he shifted to face her. His hand never leaving Lily. "It will heal. I'll take the pain if that means you aren't in danger."

"I'm not going anywhere."

"Good." Daniel rested his head on the back of the couch.

Annie had no plans to leave. In fact, Donovan Keats had visited her in the hospital last night and promised that her job would be waiting for her when she was ready to return.

A flash of black fur darted into the room. Shadow trotted to the couch, tail wagging. He nudged his wet nose against Annie's hand. She smiled and rewarded the dog with pets.

"Sorry about that." Logan stood in the doorway with his arm around Izzie's waist.

"Shadow is always welcome. He helped my baby in ways no one else could."

The pair ambled into the room and sat on the love seat.

Shadow gave a soft yip.

Lily stirred in Annie's arms, and her eyes fluttered open. "Shadow?" She rubbed her eyes. When her focus landed on the dog, she leaned forward and latched on to Shadow's neck, burying her face in his fur. "I missed you."

Daniel smiled. "He's missed you too, sweet pea."

Lily wiggled out of Annie's embrace and dropped to the floor. "Come on, boy, let's go play."

Shadow licked her cheek, which sent her into a fit of giggles. The sound was music to Annie's ears. She'd never wish for a moment of silence again. Her daughter's precious chatter hadn't returned completely, but Lily had entered the road to healing.

Her daughter and her doggy friend hurried to the blanket off to the side, but within sight of the adults. Shadow patiently lay next to Lily, allowing her to gently bounce the stuffed animals along his back.

A moment later, Izzie cleared her throat. "Besides bringing Shadow to play, Logan and I wanted to brief you on Gregory and the drug pipeline. A lot has happened over the past twenty-four hours."

Daniel held his injured arm as he shifted in his seat trying to get comfortable. That much was obvious. “How is the doctor doing?”

“I received a call about an hour ago. He didn’t make it. The doctors were confident he’d make a full recovery, but the stress on his body was too much.”

“Knowing that I killed someone doesn’t sit well. I’ll have to live with that knowledge for the rest of my life. But, I’ll admit, I’d do it again to save Annie.” He laced his fingers with hers and squeezed.

“I’m grateful for what you did. I’m just sorry it came to firing your weapon, and you getting hurt in the process.” Tears pricked her eyes. In her entire life, no one had ever sacrificed for her, and Daniel had twice. Once by shooting Gregory, leading to the man’s death, and the other by risking his life, getting shot in the process.

“Anything for you, Annie.” The tenderness in his eyes warmed her heart.

Could she hope for a future with this man? Annie let that thought go for a moment and refocused on the drug ring—pipeline—whatever they’d called it. She had given her statement last night at the hospital, so Izzie knew what Gregory had confessed, but Annie wanted to know more. She switched her attention to his sister. “Izzie, what else do you have?”

“The entire operation has been handed over to the DEA.” Izzie sighed in relief. “They’ll take over the logistics from here on out. I’m not maintaining control of the case. This goes way beyond a local bust. It’s a massive drug distribution network. Annie, I don’t think the Marshall County Sheriff’s Department or the DEA would have shut it down so quickly without you putting things in motion with Dr. Pope.”

“It seems so unreal.” Annie tried to process the past couple of weeks. “So who killed Bonner—and tried to kill me? That wasn’t Gregory.”

“No. It wasn’t.” Daniel’s jaw tightened. “The man who attacked you is named Grant. He was Gregory's dealer in the area."

"Grant's talking and is filling in some of the blanks. According to him, Gregory found out about Bonner working undercover and demanded that Grant take him out. Then Annie showed up and messed up his plans. From what we can tell, Gregory had no idea Annie moved here. His niece, Karly, didn't tell him. Karly saw an exchange between the two men that cost her her life." Izzie met Annie's gaze. "But before that happened, she hid Lily, saving your daughter, but not before he recognized her. After that, things snowballed, and Gregory got desperate. And, well, you know the rest."

All this trouble because she turned Pope over to the authorities. But the scary part? Annie would do it again even knowing the outcome. "Will they be able to shut down the operation?"

Izzie nodded. "The DEA is closing in. The pipeline starts in Mexico with the street drugs and moves through Texas, collecting hospital grade fentanyl along the way. It's a huge distribution. So far, they've discovered five doctors from four different hospitals involved. And they are still looking."

"How high up in the organization was Dr. Gregory?" Annie's stomach churned at the thought of her mentor dealing fentanyl. "I never imagined…"

Daniel gave her hand another squeeze.

"The DEA might have the lead on the case, but they've contracted GracePoint Security to help with research and the investigation. Most of us have a security clearance. What I can tell you is that we're still investigating the pipeline and the mastermind behind it." Logan tapped his fingers on his thigh. "Todd Gregory appears to have had strong ties to the Los Lobos del Desierto cartel."

Annie gasped. Would the threat ever go away?

"What is it?" Daniel asked.

"He put us in the crosshairs of a cartel?"

"No. You're safe now." Izzie motioned to Lily. "Both of you. Gregory targeted you, not the cartel."

"You're sure?"

"Absolutely." Logan added. "Breathe, Annie, it's over."

"Over?"

"Gregory can never hurt you again. The dangers to you and Lily ended with his death."

"But what about Pope?" Layton Pope's threats seemed inconsequential now, but she'd be remiss if she ignored what the man had said.

"I don't believe he'll be a problem."

She jerked her gaze to Daniel. "Why?"

"I might have made a few calls earlier today."

"And?"

"Pope has enough problems of his own. He's linked to the pipeline through Gregory. So, besides dealing with withdrawal, he's trying to save himself from bigger charges that center around his part with the cartel." Daniel fiddled with his sling. "And I might have asked a favor from a friend in San Antonio. He's promised to let me know if Pope makes any mention of you or Lily."

"Thank you. All of you. I don't know what I would have done without you."

"We were happy to help. Now, if you'll excuse us, we'll be in the kitchen with Mom." Izzie rose and Logan joined her. The couple left her and Daniel alone—minus a four-year-old and a dog.

Annie rested her head on Daniel's good shoulder. She was dying to ask where she stood in his life but refused to push. Did she want that future? Yes. But for now, she was content.

This. Right here. Right now. With the woman he'd loved in his youth and lost, resting her head on his shoulder and her daughter giggling with Shadow in the corner, Daniel had everything he'd ever dreamed of for his life. And yet, the peace he'd expected hadn't filled him. His nightmares continued to plague him, and now, he had another dark cloud hovering over him. He'd done what he had to do. He'd shot Gregory to save Annie's life. The man had been a monster—a drug dealer whose actions killed others. But the act of taking a life, no matter the circumstances—he'd carry the burden forever.

He shifted to ease the pressure on his back. The movement sent a jolt of pain through his shoulder. He tamped down a hiss but couldn't control the grimace that crossed his face. Thankfully, Annie hadn't seen it. She'd go all doctor momma bear on him. The woman could give his mom a run for her money in that department. He chuckled at the thought.

Annie lifted her face, and he got lost in her brown eyes. He'd missed her so much.

A gentle jab in his ribs brought him out of his musing. "I'm sorry, what did you say?"

"I asked what was so funny?"

"Oh." Yikes. How did he answer that? "You know me and my mind. My imagination works overtime."

"That's true." She smiled.

Daniel had found comfort here at the ranch after his academy experience. But nothing compared to Annie.

God, I'm going for it. But I can't do this alone. I want to heal. For me. For them.

He allowed the silence to stretch between him and Annie while he watched Lily playing with Shadow. Her giggles slowly chipped away at the wall of fear he had built around his heart. The girl was a light in the dark memories. A force of nature. Lily had endured more than any child should, and yet her resilience spoke volumes. Daniel could learn something from the pint-size cutie.

Yes, this was the life he'd dreamed of. He knew he'd struggle. But he was ready. He tugged Annie close and wrapped his good arm around her. "I want this, Annie," he whispered, terrified she'd turn him down after the way he'd acted. "I want you and Lily in my life. I want to build a future with you." The words were for her, but they were also a promise to himself. He refused to let his past consume him any longer. He had a reason to heal—to be whole again. That reason sat beside him. He wouldn't let her go. Not without fighting for her to stay.

Annie twisted and cupped his cheek. "Are you sure? Because I'm a package deal. Lily will be in my life forever."

"I've never been so sure of anything in my life. When your mom took you away, it left a giant hole in my heart. One only you could fill." He leaned into her touch. "If you'd have asked me about my confidence level two days ago, I'd have hesitated. But not anymore."

"What changed?"

His gaze drifted to Lily and Shadow. "That little girl over there. She did it."

"How?"

"When she found me to tell us that you needed help, she flung her arms around my neck. She trusted me to protect her. Trusted me to help you. She never questioned her safety in my arms. At that point the past didn't matter. She believed in me." He swallowed the lump in his throat. "That little munchkin not only gave me courage, but she stole my heart in that moment."

"She is pretty special."

"The most specialest little girl in the world." He gave her a cheesy grin.

Annie laughed. "I don't think most specialest is a thing. But I understand." The soft look at her daughter made him love her all the more.

The warmth spread through his chest. He laced their fingers and kissed the back of her hand. "Annie, I love you. I always have. Please, let me date you and see if we still have the same connection we did as teens."

"I don't think the connection is a problem. But I want you to be 100 percent certain that this is what you want. That Lily is what you want. I've lived a life where those who were supposed to love me threw me aside like I didn't matter. I can't do that again. And I won't do that to Lily."

"I promise. I'd never intentionally hurt you or Lily. You two mean everything to me." This time, with God's help, he'd keep his vow to the woman who'd stolen his heart years ago.

"Then, yes, Daniel. I'd love to date you. And by the way—" a smile on her lips grew "—I love you too. Always have. Always will."

His world went from muted tones to vibrant colors. A brand-new beginning for him—for them. He leaned in and brushed his lips against hers. "I'm going to hold you to that." This time, when their lips touched, he deepened the kiss, pouring his love and promise into the embrace.

God had helped him survive the dark days. But now, He'd given him the greatest gift Daniel could ask for. The woman by his side. And a little girl who'd pieced his shattered heart back together.

EPILOGUE

Thanksgiving

The scents of cinnamon and nutmeg drifting from the kitchen hung in the air. Annie followed the amazing smells. She smiled as she leaned against the doorway and watched Hannah teach Lily how to roll cookie dough and use a maple leaf cookie cutter. Laughter danced through the Stone Creek Ranch kitchen, louder than the country music playing in the background. The oven had worked overtime since Annie and Lily arrived an hour ago. The warmth mirrored the generosity and acceptance all the Sinclairs had given her and her daughter. But it was Daniel who'd made Rollins home.

"That's it, Lily-girl. Press it just enough. We want leaves, not hockey pucks." Hannah's hands guided Lily's smaller ones.

Three months ago, Annie couldn't have imagined this. Hannah had filled the role of grandmother to Lily with grace. Who was she kidding, Hannah had become a mother for her as well. Annie had known she'd missed out on a mother figure growing up. Her own had missed the mark by a mile. But it wasn't until these last few months that she understood how much of a void it had left in her life.

Izzie stood by the sink washing dishes. "How's the house coming along, Annie?"

She joined Izzie and grabbed a towel to help dry. "We're

loving it." The house she and Lily moved into after the whole Dr. Gregory debacle might be a rental, but it had become a home. "Lily loves the fenced-in backyard. Since I'm renting, I can't paint and such, but we're putting our own stamp on it where we can."

"I'm happy for you." A mischievous grin bloomed on Izzie's face. "And how's the love life?"

Heat crept up her neck. "You could ask your brother that too, you know."

"I did. He told me to ask *you*." Izzie burst out laughing.

The back door creaked open, and Daniel meandered his way into the room. He threw his arms out in a dramatic fashion. "Your daily dose of excellence just walked in."

Izzie pretended to search the room. "Where?"

"Very funny." He leaned against the edge of the counter with a smile. One that no longer masked pain but made it all the way to his eyes.

"So, you finally decided to grace us with your presence?" Izzie sniffed. "You smell like horse."

"Hey, I visited the beings that love me the most first."

Annie quirked a brow. She loved seeing Daniel's playful side. "Your horse doesn't count."

"Aspen disagrees."

Lily finally spotted him and bolted off the step stool she'd used to reach the countertop. "Mr. Daniel! You came!"

"Of course I did, squirt." He caught her mid-leap, spun her around, and set her on her feet. "Wouldn't miss Thanksgiving with my two favorite girls."

Lily placed her hands on her hips, perfectly mimicking Annie. "What about Aunt Izzie and Grandma Hannah?"

Daniel beamed at her choice of words. "Okay, okay. Four favorite girls. But you and your mom have a special place right here." He tapped his chest.

Tears pooled on Annie's lashes. When she'd first arrived,

she'd never imagined being here with this family and dating Daniel.

Hannah wiped her hands and clapped. "Let's get this show on the road. Cooper, Grace, and Lexi will be here in a few minutes. The table's set. Would someone please call Payton in from the barn?" The older woman spun and faced Izzie. "And where's that husband of yours?"

"Right here, Mom." Logan and Shadow stood in the doorway of the kitchen. "What can I help with?"

Hannah pointed to the platter of turkey. "Take that and put it on the table."

"Yes, ma'am." Logan snuck a piece before doing what he'd been told. And got a towel snapped at him for his unauthorized bite.

"I'll grab Payton." Daniel hurried out the door.

What was that man up to?

Cooper, Grace, and Lexi arrived just in time. Dinner passed in a blur of chaos. Once everyone helped clear the table, they gathered in the living room.

Lexi, Cooper and Grace's daughter, played with Lily and Shadow by the fireplace while conversations overlapped and stories flew. Shadow's tail thumped against the floor with all the attention the girls lavished on him.

Daniel nudged her. "You know she loves that dog, right?"

Annie rested her head on his shoulder. "She does, but Logan needs him. Lily has visiting rights, so they play together often."

Payton sat crossed-legged on the floor next to the couch. "You know, you could get Lily a dog of her own. You've got that great backyard."

Daniel glared at his sister.

What was his problem?

Lily tugged Annie's sleeve. "Can we go for a walk? Please? I want to see the barn. Mr. Daniel promised."

Annie narrowed her eyes at Daniel, who tried and failed to look innocent. "I guess so."

"Come on. Let's go." Lily hurried to the back door.

Annie grabbed a jacket and followed Daniel and Lily into the crisp afternoon air.

"What is she up to?"

Daniel shrugged but didn't comment.

Those two had something up their sleeves. A smile pulled at her lips. Her daughter and Daniel. Who would have ever thought they'd become attached in such a short time? And for that alone, she'd give thanks.

Daniel filled his lungs with the crisp fall air, clearing the unease wrapped around him. This was it. The moment he'd waited for all day. Now, if he could get through the surprises for both his girls and neither hated his gifts for them. He laced his fingers with Annie's. Her touch alone settled his heart and mind. The three of them strolled across the back lawn toward the barn.

The minute they hit the gravel outside the entrance, Lily flung the door open and made a beeline for Aspen. She pressed her cheek to the horse's nose. Aspen bobbed his head up and down. But unlike with Daniel, the horse gentled his movement.

"I think you might be in danger of losing your horse's loyalty." Annie laughed.

"Nah, Aspen's loyal to a fault. Although I have to admit, those two have forged an unbreakable friendship."

"So it appears."

He wrapped his arm around Annie's waist and watched the child and beast. "You know, one of these days that girl will need her own horse."

"And where do you propose we keep it? I live in town. Granted, my backyard is a good size, but not horse size."

"Hmm, well, then, maybe we start with something a bit smaller."

"Daniel Thomas Sinclair, what did you do?"

Wow, she really could read his mind. A smile split his face. "I don't know what you're talking about. I'm innocent."

"Right. Suuuure you are." Annie shook her head.

Daniel released Annie and strode to Lily. He picked up the little one and dropped her over his shoulder. It felt good to no longer have to baby his arm. The injury had healed nicely with no lasting issues. Life was good and about to get better. He grinned as he carried Lily toward the tack room. A bark echoed from the other side of the door.

"What was that?" Annie asked.

Daniel shrugged. If he said anything, he'd ruin the surprise.

He dropped Lily to her feet and opened the door. Inside, a young Bernese mountain dog stood behind a wire fenced-in area similar to a playpen. His tail wagged hard enough to knock him off balance. Ears perked, his eyes locked on to Lily. Unlike Shadow, this fellow had thick black fur with white-and-brown accents.

Lily gasped. "A doggy!"

"Go ahead. He's well behaved." He opened the gate. The dog bounded out of his entrapment and skidded to a stop in front of Lily. His pink tongue licked a strip up her cheek.

Giggles burst from the young girl. She sat on the ground and loved on the dog.

"You know, he needs a name."

"I can name him?" Lily bounced.

"Yes. But take your time. It has to be a good one." Daniel winked at Annie.

He witnessed the moment she realized what was happening. Her hand flew to her mouth and tears welled in her eyes.

"Jasper," Lily announced seconds later.

The dog yipped.

"I think he likes it." Annie's eyes hadn't left her daughter.

"Well, that was fast. So, what do you think, Jasper? Do you like your new name?"

The dog barked.

Daniel chuckled. "Then it's official."

"Oh, Jasper, I love you." Lily practically strangled the dog, but Jasper didn't seem to mind.

Annie's gaze met his.

"Well?" Daniel held his breath.

She sniffed and nodded.

"Lily, a buddy of mine has been training Jasper. He does the same job as Shadow. I think he'd like to be your dog."

"Mine?" Lily's big eyes blinked at him.

"Yes, yours. Assuming it's okay with your momma."

"Momma, can I please have Jasper? Please?"

Annie sighed, wiping her cheek. "How can I say no? Of course you can keep him."

"Yay! I love him so much! Thank you, Mr. Daniel!"

"I can't believe you did that for her," Annie said.

"Figured she needed a dog that's just hers. Shadow was great, but temporary. This guy? He's permanent. And as an added bonus, he's well trained. So that shouldn't be a problem."

Mission one accomplished. Daniel's heart thudded in his chest. Time for part two.

"Hey, squirt." He crouched beside Lily. "Can Jasper and you hang out for a bit? I want to talk to your mom for a minute."

Lily nodded but didn't glance up. She was nose deep in dog fluff, oblivious to the world around her.

Daniel clasped Annie's hand and led her to the main room of the barn. Gold rays of sunlight filtered through hinged barn windows in each stall, giving him hope. He turned to face her, every nerve in his body lit up like a Christmas tree on Christmas day.

"Annie." He cleared the emotion from his throat. "When you left Rollins, I never thought I'd be whole again. But by God's grace, you came back—and not just to town. You came back to me. You saved me from drowning in guilt and regret. You were patient with me when you didn't have to be."

Heart hammering, he reached into his coat pocket and pulled out the ring box. He dropped to one knee.

Annie sucked in a breath. Her eyes shimmered.

"You and Lily…you're my heart. I want to build a future with the two of you. Will you marry me, Annie? Make us a real family?"

She clapped a hand over her mouth, then dropped to her knees in front of him. "Oh, Daniel. I've wanted you my whole life. Yes, I'll marry you."

He slipped the princess cut diamond on her finger.

She admired the ring for a moment, then cupped his face and kissed him.

Resting his forehead against her, he smiled. "You know, since I have a house on the edge of Stone Creek Ranch, I think we might have enough room for that horse for Lily."

"Daniel Sinclair, behave yourself." She patted his cheek. "Let's start with the dog and go from there."

"Did you do it, Mr. Daniel? Did you ask her?" Lily peeked out of the tack room with Jasper by her side.

Annie's mouth dropped open. "You asked a four-year-old if it was okay to propose?" she whispered.

"Of course I did. She's your daughter."

Annie wiped her eyes and laughed. "He did."

Lily ran over. "And?"

One arm around Annie, he scooped Lily into a hug with the other. "And your mom said yes."

"Yay!" Lily squealed. "I get a dog and a daddy!"

The air squeezed from Daniel's lungs. "Daddy?"

Lily grinned and nodded. "I want you to be my daddy, if that's okay."

"I'd love nothing more." Daniel blinked away the tears threatening to fall and closed his eyes.

Thank You, God, for bringing Annie back to me. And giving me the gift of a life with these two.

Annie rested her head on his shoulder as Jasper sat and pushed against his leg.

He finally had it all.

Home. Family. Love.

* * * * *

If you enjoyed this book in Sami A. Abrams's Stone Creek Ranch miniseries, be sure to pick up these previous titles:

Christmas Rodeo Killer
Deadly Rodeo Threat

Available now from Love Inspired Suspense!

Dear Reader,

Thank you for reading *Rodeo Witness Protector*, book three in the Stone Creek Ranch miniseries. I hope you enjoy getting to know Daniel and Annie. Painful pasts are hard to move on from, but with God and someone you love by your side, anything is possible.

I'd like to send a shout-out to my awesome agent, Tamela Hancock Murray, and to my amazing editor, Shana Asaro. You two are the best! I absolutely love working with you. And thank you to my Suspense Squad girls. Knowing there's a group of writers who I can call at any time for writing help or just to laugh is amazing. Thank you, ladies. And to my writing community—you're wonderful.

Let's not forget a special thank-you to my law enforcement consultant, Detective James Williams, Sacramento Internet Crimes Against Children, who answers all my crazy questions. By the way, all mistakes are my own or are author privileges, so don't complain to him. Lol!

And thank you to my family for their love and support. Love you bunches, Darren, Matthew, and Melissa!

I hope you enjoyed reading Daniel and Annie's story. If you'd like a BONUS SCENE, go to my website, samiaabrams.com.

I'd love to hear from you. You can contact me through my website where you can also sign up for my newsletter to receive exclusive subscriber news and giveaways.

Hugs,
Sami A. Abrams